Fairford Affairs

BOOK 1

FIXING Olivia

BAY SINCLAIR

Fixing Olivia

Copyright © 2023 by Bay Sinclair

All rights reserved.

To Jason, for bringing an endless supply of joy to my life.

And to Carla and Kelly, for being my number one fans from the very beginning.

CHAPTER 1

Aiden

Thank Christ, she was finally fucking leaving.

Aiden plastered a smile on his face and waved as the Mercedes drove down the driveway. He kept it up until the small white coupe had passed through the open front gates and out of sight. Dropping his arm, he closed his eyes and sighed. That had *not* been an easy week, and he was relieved to see the last of Stacey Blackwood.

He really had to stop taking heiresses and the like as guests. People who grew up getting everything they ever wanted didn't understand what it meant to truly submit to someone. Not in any of the ways that mattered. Though of course they thought they did, and how could they possibly ever be wrong? And he was oh so tired of his lifestyle being treated like some kind of kinky game.

Two days into her weeklong stay, he'd wanted nothing more than to send Stacey packing. But since their business depended almost solely on word of mouth, the others would be furious with him if they found out he'd even considered it.

Giving his shoulders a roll, Aiden forced his eyes to reopen and headed to the house. Vermont in January was no joke, but even the sting of the cold against his skin didn't inspire him to move quickly. He practically trudged up the steps to the double front doors.

His plan was to head straight upstairs, grab his stuff, and go. He had three whole days off, and he wanted to spend them alone, with no snippy little subs trying to top from the bottom in their nasally, whiny-ass voices.

Okay, he was *really fucking relieved* to have seen the last of Stacey Blackwood.

Maybe they should start doing video applications. If he could look into their eyes and watch how they chose to present themselves, then he'd get a feel for potential guests' attitude, their bearing, their spirit. He'd know if they were truly submissive by nature, or if they liked to read naughty novels and thought a few playful spankings and a butt plug would be a great way to unwind.

And he'd know if the sound of their voice would be like nails on a chalkboard, torturing him for days on end.

"So. How'd it go."

It wasn't really a question, and when Aiden turned toward the front desk, he wasn't surprised to see Zach smirking at him.

Zach was Fairford Manor's office manager/concierge/reception-ist/marketing expert/bookkeeper/basically everything else under the sun. He may have favored vests and bow ties over camouflage, but that didn't stop him from running the whole place with military precision.

Aiden didn't quite understand why the guy wanted to work at a BDSM resort if he never took any guests. Even their chef had allowed a couple sous chefs and one particularly talented pastry chef to submit in his kitchen. But he wasn't about to complain. Everything ran so much smoother with Zach there, and the guests loved him.

Rolling his eyes at Zach's smug expression, Aiden said, "Oh, it was great. Best damn week of my life."

"I could tell." The younger man was clearly trying hard not to laugh. "Especially the way your left eye started twitching every time she spoke by day three."

"Video applications." Aiden gave an exaggerated wink when Zach pretended to gasp. "Genius, right? It's the new frontier."

Chuckling, Zach said, "I'm sure that's exactly what all our potential guests want—videos of them begging to be dominated that might someday show up on the internet."

Aiden gave him a rueful smile. "There you go with your damn logic again."

"I know, I know. One of my many faults."

Some of the tension in Aiden's shoulders fell away. How did Zach always know how to calm him down or cheer him up when things with the guests went south? He did the same for the subs whenever they needed it. The man was seriously a godsend.

He made a mental note to make Jonathan—who was technically in charge, and had final say on all decisions at the Manor—give him a raise.

"Don't worry," Zach said, leaning back in his chair. "I just spoke to your next guest on the phone. Her voice is sexy as hell. You're gonna love it."

"Thank God for small miracles," Aiden said, trying to at least *sound* happy, even if his heart wasn't in it.

The words came out with all the excitement you'd hear at a funeral.

Zach's eyes narrowed. "You okay, man?"

"Never better," Aiden lied, turning toward the stairs so Zach couldn't see his face. "I'll go grab my stuff so I'm not in housekeeping's way."

"Off to your cabin for the weekend?"

"You know it," he called over his shoulder. His cabin was the only place he could let his guard down and relax these days. It was so draining to be *on* all the time—to constantly be in full-blown Dom mode. How the others managed it without the slightest sign of strain was beyond him.

Planning and prepping for scenes had always given him so much pleasure, ever since he'd stumbled into the lifestyle in college. Bringing those plans to fruition with a sub who made his cock ache with need? Nothing in the world could compare. But now it was just . . . well, *work*.

He rolled his eyes at his own train of thought. You turn something you love into a job, and it feels like work. Wow. Go figure. With brilliant insights like that, he should've gotten his degree in philosophy instead of business.

Leo would understand.

The errant thought had him pulling out his phone as he entered the suite Stacey had vacated minutes before. After typing and deleting three different messages, though, he gave up and slid the phone back into his pocket.

Leo definitely *would* understand. Hell, the man had run off and married his childhood sweetheart soon after they'd bought the mansion, before the Manor even opened to guests. If anyone could give him advice about how exhausting it had all become—about this new, creeping desire to do something *real* with his life—it would be Leo.

But he'd probably also tell Jonathan. The two of them had been roommates and best friends in college, leaving Aiden and the others always just outside their innermost circle. And the last thing he needed right now was Fairford Manor's senior partner breathing down his neck, making everything even more stressful.

Aiden tossed his things into a small duffel bag with a little more force than was entirely necessary. Closing his eyes, he made himself take several deep breaths. What was he even so upset about? So he had a shitty client. Big deal. It happened to all of them now and again. At least it wasn't like those first two years, while they were trying to get the business on its feet. He cringed as he remembered some of their worst kink mismatches.

But now Fairford Manor was well-known, its name spoken everywhere from clubs and hardcore dungeons to the most casual of BDSM munches. There was even a subreddit where subs who'd visited the Manor gave all the dirty details to the women who dreamed of one day being selected. (Which Zach had started, of course, though no one knew that.)

That very moment, there were dozens of applications up in an office on the third floor, just waiting for him. He was living his fucking dream.

So why did a tiny part of him miss life before the Manor, when he'd been flipping houses for a living? At least *that* had felt real. And his scenes back then . . .

With a sigh, he trekked back down the long hallway that ran the length of the second floor. When they'd bought the mansion six years earlier, there had been twelve bedrooms and half as many bathrooms crammed onto the top two levels. But they'd spent a year (and a hell of a lot of Jonathan, Leo, and Mason's money, plus every meager penny

Aiden had) gutting the dilapidated building and turning it into their perfect little sex haven.

Now the second floor held five stunning suites, each with its own cavernous bathroom. Along with the application room, there were several bedrooms on the third floor—for the Doms to sleep in when their guests needed space—plus a break room that boasted the only TV in the house.

He ran his fingertips along the chair rail as he headed toward the stairs. With all the massive changes they'd made, it had been a pain in the ass to keep the original, hand-carved woodwork throughout the house. But Aiden had been the general contractor on the remodel, and he'd made it his top priority to preserve or restore as much of the mansion's old-world charm as possible. No matter how sick and tired he got of bad guests, at least seeing what he'd transformed this building into made him proud every damn day.

Maybe that was the problem. There was nothing for him to fix anymore.

As Aiden passed one of the other suites, a low, keening moan drifted through the door, followed by, "Sir, *please* let me come. I'll be a good girl, I swear!"

Something stirred deep in Aiden's core. There were few things he loved more than a submissive begging in a husky, sex-saturated voice. God, he hoped his next guest had a voice like that. Repressing a groan, he forced himself to leave Camden—one of the other Doms now in residence—to his fun, and hurried down the wide, curving staircase.

It was time for three full days of peace and quiet, and then maybe he'd get his own turn to play with a woman who heated his blood with passion instead of annoyance. A woman who would submit to him for the sole reason that doing so made her feel whole—not so she could force him to spank her when she decided disobedience was way more fun.

"Hey, grab your mail on your way by," Zach called out as Aiden reached the lobby. "I just tried to put a few more letters in your box, but it was full."

Not holding his groan back this time, he redirected his steps toward the little office behind the reception desk. Some of the other guys absolutely loved getting what Aiden referred to as their fan mail. Especially Camden. The man couldn't get enough of it, the fucking horndog. But Aiden found it awkward as hell, especially when the letters were downright pornographic, complete with nude photos.

If only Jonathan would let him throw the mail away without opening it. But alas, repeat customers were a huge part of their business. Anything to keep the guests happy and dying to return, right?

Grabbing a stack of envelopes, magazines, and junk from his mailbox, he hurried outside before anything else could delay him, giving Zach a quick wave on his way by. He strode down the flagstone path to the parking lot as quickly as his long legs could carry him without legit running. He only hoped it looked like he wanted to get out of the cold, and not like he was running away.

When at last he settled behind the driver's seat of his Land Rover, he sighed, his breath fogging the frigid winter air. No one would try to stop him now. And the gray clouds filling the sky looked like they had snow in them. Maybe he'd get snowed in up at his cabin, or his next guest's flight would be cancelled.

Or maybe it was time for a longer break than a few days. He hadn't had a proper vacation in over six years, for Christ's sake. No wonder he was completely burned out.

Tossing the stack of mail onto the passenger seat, Aiden started the car and put it into reverse. But before he could take his foot off the brake, he noticed a manila envelope that had been hidden between two magazines, the front completely blank. He plucked it from the pile and checked the back, which was also free of the usually necessary things like addresses or postage. The top flap wasn't even sealed.

"What the hell?" he muttered, throwing the car into park and opening the envelope. What he pulled out made his eyebrows shoot up toward his hairline. It was an application.

By company policy, all applications were put into their respective stacks up in the application room, for each Dom to peruse at his leisure. Zach read through them first, sorting them into categories ranging from Curious Newbie to Pain Slut, M/s Fantasy to Pet Play. Never had one been given directly to him.

"Fucking Zach," Aiden said, turning the car off. The man must've

6

sorted it into his mail by mistake, and now he had to walk all the way back across the yard and inside to return it. If Jonathan pulled him into a meeting, or Rafe wanted to discuss dungeon upgrades again, he was going to scream.

But as he reached for the door handle, a phrase on the bottom of the first page caught his eye: *I think it's the only way to fix me.*

Aiden's hand clenched involuntarily, wrinkling the thick packet of paper. *"Shit."* He smoothed it out against his thigh, his hands shaking slightly with a sudden adrenaline rush.

Not even taking the time to turn the car's heater back on, Aiden started reading the application from the beginning.

CHAPTER 2
Olivia

"You do realize it's Friday, right?" Jen's wheedling voice came through the car's speakers.

Olivia rolled her eyes. The accounting firm where she worked had been short-staffed since 2020, and she'd just finished yet another red-letter week in her career. The last thing she wanted was to have the same irritating conversation for the ten thousandth time.

"Shockingly enough, I'm well aware of what day it is," Olivia replied, trying to sound amused rather than annoyed. It sort of worked.

"But you never go out," Jen said, her tone going from wheedling to straight-up whining. "You wouldn't even come celebrate your birthday last weekend. *Please?* It'll be fun."

Olivia couldn't keep herself from laughing. Yeah, she didn't go out because none of her friends bothered to ask what *she* wanted to do—on her own damn birthday. "When has it ever been fun?" Before Jen could get out more than a word of her objection, she added a curt, "For me?"

The line went quiet for so long, Olivia glanced at the car's display to see if the call had disconnected. But no, her friend's name and picture still glowed on the small screen. Jen only got quiet like this when her feelings were hurt.

Olivia repressed a sigh, forcing herself not to give voice to the apology on the tip of her tongue. Jen should be the one apologizing, for harassing her to go out *every damn weekend* as if the answer would somehow change. Part of her even felt like maybe her friendship with Jen had run its course—that they were such different people now than when they'd met, and the two of them no longer made sense.

Not that any of the other people in their friend group were different. If she ditched them all, who else would she have? The last thing she needed was to feel more alone than she already did.

"Look, I know bars and clubs and dancing with super-hot guys is your thing," Olivia said, softening her voice. "And I think that's great . . . for you. Honestly, I wish I found all that fun. My life would be a hell of a lot more interesting. But it makes me anxious as all hell. I'm sorry."

Jen was quiet for a few more seconds—long enough to ensure Olivia knew she was still unhappy. Then she heaved the dramatic sigh Olivia had kept in. "You think I don't know that?"

Olivia frowned as she navigated her car toward the back of the apartment complex. "Then why—"

"Because it seems like you've given up on you. And I don't want to give up on you, too."

Okay, Olivia was definitely back to being annoyed. "I've given up on me because I like reading or watching TV more than I like grinding up against some rando on the dance floor?" She couldn't have kept the sarcasm out of her voice if she'd tried.

"When's the last time you had sex?" Jen demanded.

Olivia was very glad she'd just parked, because God only knows what would've happened if the car had been in motion. "I—that's—what does that even matter?" she spluttered.

"Or been on a date or whatever," Jen said, with an annoyed little huff. "I know you get all squicky about casual hookups. Are you even on any dating sites?"

She had been. Once upon a time. But the kind of men she met on those sites did absolutely nothing for her. At least not in the bedroom. And the one guy she'd liked and trusted enough to open up to about what she needed had ghosted her the very next day. She'd long since decided her time was way too precious to keep wasting it, and closed all her accounts.

Not that she could explain any of that to Jen in a way she'd understand. So she found herself going on the offensive instead. "And which of your sexy one-night stands has turned into a lasting relationship?"

Jen's laugh was harsh. "Are you seriously slut shaming me?"

"Jesus, of course not." Olivia pressed her head against the headrest and closed her eyes until she'd calmed down a little. "I've known you for eight years. When, in all that time, have I ever given a fuck who you sleep with? I'm just saying, if you know I prefer dating to hookups, why do you keep trying to make me go out with you when you're *only* looking for hookups?"

Another sigh came through the car speakers. "I know. I'm sorry. I don't know what's gotten into me lately. I think . . ." Jen groaned, then forced out, "I think I'm probably freaking out about turning thirty next month."

Olivia had to hold in what she knew was a dismissive reply. Her own thirtieth birthday had come and gone three years earlier, and she hadn't noticed or cared. But then her age had never really mattered to her the way it did to her friends. They all thought if you didn't have your entire life figured out by thirty, sucks to be you, time was officially up.

"I know, it's tough," she said, trying to sound appropriately empathetic. "But hey, on the bright side, you don't look a day older than twenty-two."

Jen's appreciative chuckle was a tiny bit smug. "That's true."

"Happy hunting tonight."

"Thanks." She even sounded like she meant it. "Have a nice time with your Kindle."

"You know it."

When the call disconnected, Olivia closed her eyes again and let herself breathe for several seconds. She'd been on edge before the call, but now, her heart and mind were both racing. If only she'd been brave enough to tell Jen what she'd done. It would've helped to have someone to talk to about her dumbass decision to send an application to the infamous Fairford Manor last weekend. It might've even gotten Jen off her back about the whole sex/dating thing.

But the few careful feelers Olivia had put out about BDSM to her sex-loving friend had always been met with a response that was anything but positive. She was one of those women who skipped over the *consensual* part of the definition, labeling everything within the lifestyle as abuse. As if she knew anything about it.

Though admittedly, Olivia didn't know anything from firsthand experience either. Sure, like any wannabe sub, she'd gotten plenty familiar with Ye Olde Google, obsessing over the websites of BDSM clubs around the world, scrolling through picture galleries and imagining herself in the different dungeons. She'd even bought herself a few sexy outfits—clothes that would hopefully project to any unattached Dom in the room that she was a sub looking to play.

But the few times her daydreams had turned into concrete plans, she'd always been too chickenshit to go through with it. If she'd had someone to go with her, it would've been a whole different story. Especially if that person was active on the scene themselves and could show her the ropes. Help her understand the unspoken rules. Make sure she didn't make a fucking idiot of herself in front of a roomful of people, because everything she knew about BDSM came from kinky novels.

Hence her application to Fairford Manor. There, she wouldn't have to attract a Dom and try to keep his attention as she awkwardly stumbled through all sorts of unknown steps. He'd already know she was a total newbie from her application, without her having to explain it verbally. Her throat would probably close up from sheer embarrassment if she ever tried.

It had seemed like a faaaaabulous idea on her birthday, after a bottle and a half of cabernet sauvignon. Less so now.

With a deep sigh, Olivia grabbed her keys and purse, heading inside. It wasn't like any of the Doms would pick her anyway. She knew from lurking on the subreddit devoted to the Manor that the place was Exclusive with a capital E. They wouldn't pick a thirty-three-year-old with no experience and anxiety.

Besides, the wine had made her *way* too honest on her application. She might as well have written, *I HAD A SHIT CHILDHOOD AND NOW I'M BROKEN—NO FUN TO BE HAD HERE!* in big block letters on the first page. So why waste her time worrying about it?

Because worrying was what Olivia did best.

Olivia grabbed her mail on her way through the lobby, tucking the stack of envelopes and ads under her arm, and headed up to her second-floor apartment. Her *empty* second-floor apartment. No boyfriend, no roommate. Not even a pet.

Yeah, that was the answer to all her problems. Time to accept she'd be alone forever and get a fucking cat.

Frustrated, she threw her keys, purse, and mail onto her dining room table, then stalked into the kitchen to check if she had any of that birthday wine left. Score one for the depressed chick: half a bottle of the cab waited in her fridge door, and there was an unopened bottle of merlot in her otherwise empty wine rack. Perfection. It was easier to lose herself in her deliciously naughty books if she was slightly drunk. Easier to imagine she was the heroine who'd finally met her perfect Dom.

Glass of wine in hand, Olivia headed toward her living room, stopping on the way to grab her Kindle from her purse. That was when she noticed the bit of textured ivory cardstock peeking out between the other pieces of scattered mail. Pulling it free from the pile, Olivia groaned when she saw the fine calligraphy on the front of the obviously expensive envelope.

Just what she needed, another wedding invite. So she could sit around with all her married college friends and talk about their children and the fancy vacations they went on, and how all of them clearly had better lives than her.

Well, except for the ones who were already divorced. She'd actually enjoyed the one wedding where her table was full of semi-recent divorcees. Better to be eternally single than to go through that total shitshow.

Olivia was going to toss the invite back into the pile and worry about it the next day. But curiosity got the better of her before she could turn away. She might as well check the return address and find out who was tying the knot.

Flipping the envelope over, she read the two lines of delicately scrawled calligraphy on the back flap. And she very nearly dropped her glass of wine.

Fairford, VT

She'd actually gotten a reply from the Manor? It had to be some kind of mistake. Or maybe it was a polite rejection letter. *We're sorry, but you do not meet any of our Dominants' needs. We wish you all the best in your search for submissive bliss.* Yeah, that had to be it.

Her hand shook as she put down her glass, sending ripples across the surface of the wine. "Calm the fuck down," she scolded, taking a couple of deep breaths. She absolutely refused to have a panic attack over mail. Then, holding her breath, she slipped her finger under the flap and gently pried it loose.

There was a single piece of paper inside, every bit as fancy and expensive as the envelope. She unfolded it before she could chicken out yet again, and her gaze hungrily skipped past the formal header, straight to the body of the letter.

Dear Ms. Adams,

Thank you for your interest in Fairford Manor. We are delighted to inform you that we have upcoming vacancies at the resort and are looking forward to your stay. Your host during your visit will be Mr. Aiden McLaren, who is very much looking forward to making your acquaintance.

Please call the number above to arrange the details of your upcoming trip. I will be all too happy to personally assist you in finding the dates and vacation package that work best for you.

Be advised that cell phones and other recording devices are not permitted on Manor property. A list of additional rules and restrictions will be provided once you book your stay. Feel free to reach out with any questions or concerns.

Best regards,

Zachary Potter

Olivia stared at the page, trying to make the lovely, curvy handwriting make sense. Where was the apology? The polite-but-clearly-bullshit reason why they were rejecting her? That was the only outcome she'd been prepared for.

Obviously, she couldn't actually *go* to a fancy-ass kink resort . . . could she? For one thing, it would set her back quite a bit on the down payment she was saving up for. Though the housing market was crap right now anyway, so maybe that wasn't a dealbreaker. Even so, it would be irresponsible as all hell. And Olivia Adams simply didn't do irresponsible.

Besides, the people who went to Fairford Manor were outgoing, sexy, exciting. The most exciting part of her day had been figuring out why the numbers were off in one of her client's accounts. Hell, one of the few times she'd gone clubbing with her friends, she'd almost started hyperventilating when a guy asked her if she wanted to head over to his place.

But to pass up Fairford Manor . . . talk about something you'd regret until the day you died.

Reasons why she should and shouldn't go spiraled in her mind, until she couldn't even form a coherent thought. Jesus fucking Christ, she *was* going to have a panic attack over mail.

Grabbing an anxiety pill from her purse, she downed it with a gulp of wine. Closing her eyes, she waited until the thoughts racing through her head at breakneck speed slowed to a gentle stroll, until her heart beat at a normal pace. Only then did she read the letter again.

She'd been chosen. She hadn't imagined it. And by Aiden-fucking-McLaren—one of the original founders, who the girls on Reddit called the Hunk with a Heart. If anyone could ease her into the lifestyle without setting off the innumerable alarm bells that had always stopped her before, it had to be him.

Was she really going to pass that up because—why? Cause accountants were supposed to be too boring to fuck outside the box?

Fuck. That.

The second it clicked into place she was actually going, she screamed so loudly her neighbor banged on their adjoining wall.

CHAPTER 3
Aiden

"Umm, excuse you. Why are you getting mud all over my desk exactly?"

Aiden gave Zach an apologetic little wave, but his gaze stayed completely focused on Zach's computer monitor. "I'll leave in a minute," he said, only half paying attention to what he was saying.

With a disgusted sound deep in his throat, Zach reached over the reception counter to shove Aiden's feet off the surface of his desk. "I'm going to get some wet paper towels. I expect you to be gone when I get back."

Aiden gave another distracted wave, though he hadn't actually heard a word Zach said. He was completely focused on the image on the screen, which showed the security footage from the front gates.

A dark blue Ford SUV was parked about ten feet away from the camera. The woman inside was hunched over her steering wheel, shoulders rising and falling rapidly. He hadn't yet seen her face.

"Were you even listening to me?" Zach demanded.

Glancing up only long enough to see the mound of dripping paper towels in Zach's hand and the annoyed tilt of his eyebrows, Aiden gave an honest, "Not really, no."

Zach snorted. "I appreciate your honesty. I think."

In answer, Aiden pointed at the screen. "Look."

Curiosity quickened Zach's steps as he came around the counter, and he leaned over Aiden's shoulder for a closer look. "Huh." Plopping the wad of paper towels down onto the desk, he shuffled through a stack of files before pulling one out.

Aiden recognized the folder immediately, as it was much more worn than the others in the pile. Olivia's application was in there, including her list of hard and soft limits, fantasies and fears, test results proving she was clean, and everything else her new Dom would want to know. He'd taken to reading through it whenever he had a little downtime, until he'd all but memorized her file.

Zach dug through the folder for a few seconds, pulling out a parking pass with the Bronco's license plate number written on it. "That seems to be the car of your next guest."

As if Aiden needed the confirmation. He'd recognized her hair's loose black curls the moment he'd seen her. He'd been imagining running his fingers through that hair ever since he saw the picture in her application. "Indeed."

"I hate to say it," Zach said, "but your next guest *appears* to be having a panic attack."

"So it would seem." And he had no idea what to do about it. If a sub got overwhelmed during a scene, he knew exactly how to handle it. That was literally his job, and he was damn good at it. But Olivia hadn't even driven onto Manor property, let alone checked in. He wasn't in charge yet. And he didn't much care for the feeling.

Zach straightened the pile with Olivia's file, then fiddled with his bow tie, as if it wasn't already perfectly straight. The man always looked even more put together than Jonathan or Mason, and that was saying something. Finally, he took a deep breath and said, "I know we have a no refund policy, but given the circumstances, I think we should make an exception."

Aiden's gaze snapped up to Zach's so fast he tweaked a muscle in his neck. "She will *not* be asking for a refund."

People usually got nervous when Aiden stared them down like that. They'd fidget and look away, or even take a step back. But Zach had known Aiden too long for that. He stared right back into his eyes and arched a single eyebrow. "Not sure that's up to you, man. Look at the poor girl."

With a huff of annoyance, Aiden stood and walked away. There was no point trying to explain it to the younger man. He wouldn't understand. Olivia *needed* him.

It had been more than six months since he'd first read her application—and had the acceptance letter sent out that very same morning. Aiden had no idea why she'd booked so far out; it wasn't as if he hadn't had earlier vacancies. But Olivia Adams had been on his mind for half a year, and he wasn't going to let her give up when she was so close to getting what her body so desperately longed for.

"Don't get us sued and make good choices!" Zach called after him in a singsong voice.

Aiden ignored him completely, hurrying outside to the sweltering June heat before the warning even died away. He only hesitated for a second at the edge of the covered farmer's porch, enjoying a last moment in the shade while he ensured there were no blue SUVs heading for the parking lot.

Hurrying down the porch steps, he cut straight across the sweeping front lawn, not wasting time with the pathway. It took only a few minutes for his long legs to carry him out to the front gates.

He took a moment to compose himself right at the end of the driveway. It was so humid, even that short walk had made his T-shirt stick to his skin, and he knocked a new batch of mud off his shoes. Schooling his expression into the perfect Dom face that made true submissives fall to their knees, he passed through the stone pillars and faced the blue Ford.

Olivia was still hunched over her steering wheel, but at least her shoulders had stopped that far-too-rapid rise and fall. That was a good sign. As he got closer to the car, he could hear her muttering to herself through the cracked windows. It took until he was right next to her door to understand the low words.

" . . .fuck, fuck, fuck, *fuck*. Come on, get your shit together. You can do this, you can do this, you can fucking *do* this. He picked you. You told him everything and he still picked you. *So calm the fuck down.* Fuck, fuck, fuck, fuck, fu—"

19

Pulling her car door open, Aiden interrupted the flow of obsceni-ties: "I don't allow that kind of language from my subs."

Olivia's squeak of surprise was downright inhuman. Her head shot up, gaze locking onto his, while her mouth moved like it was trying to find words. No more sound came out.

It took every bit of self-control he had not to smile. Christ, she was adorable. "What seems to be the problem, Olivia?" he asked, voice firm.

Her mouth opened and closed a few more times, like an extremely cute and distraught fish, before she finally managed to gasp out, *"Aiden."*

Aiden's cock hardened at the sound of his name in her breathy voice. And that's what she sounded like after only a few stern words. He could only imagine how goddamn sexy she would be in the throes of an actual scene.

If he had his druthers, she'd be bent over the seat with his cock filling her pussy in ten seconds flat. But this week was supposed to be about her—*her* needs. Pushing aside his still-rising lust for now, he hard-ened his voice even more and said, "Is that an appropriate way to address your Dom?"

Olivia clapped a hand over her mouth, her eyes going wide. "Oh, I'm sorry. I mean no, Sir, it isn't."

He gave her the tiniest nod of approval. "Better. But I'm afraid we're off to a bit of a rocky start." Color immediately flooded her cheeks, but she didn't look away from him. Combined with the little pep talk he'd overheard, he couldn't help admiring her courage. "In addition to what we've already discussed, I've been waiting for you in the Manor for more than twenty minutes. I don't like to be kept wait-ing, Olivia."

She blinked back tears. "I'm sorry, Sir. I tried to be on time."

"So I noticed." He gave the security camera on the front gates a pointed look, and she followed his gaze, making another little squeaking sound when she saw it pointing right at her. "You actually would've been early if you hadn't stopped out here. What happened?"

Olivia closed her eyes, and a single tear made its way down her cheek. Christ, her skin looked soft. Needing to touch her, Aiden reached out and wiped the tear away with his thumb. Her lips parted in the softest of sighs at the contact. Straightening her shoulders, she made herself look at him again. "I'm scared, Sir."

He kept his face impassive. "Of?"

"Of not knowing what I'm supposed to do. Of making a mistake. Of . . ." She took a deep, steadying breath, and forced out in a smaller voice, "Of not being able to please you, Sir."

Nothing surprising there. Her explanation echoed what he'd read in her application. "Let me explain something to you," Aiden said, softening his voice the tiniest bit. "We get hundreds of applications. Most of them are experienced subs looking for something new. Something exciting and luxurious to brag to all their friends at the local club about."

"I know, Sir," she said, voice shaking. "That's why I'm so—"

"Another strike, Olivia. Don't interrupt me when I'm speaking."

Her eyes widened again, but she didn't say a word.

"Good girl. Now, where was I? The point I'm trying to make is if I wanted a sub with tons of experience, who knew exactly what she was doing, I would've picked one. I'm hardly lacking in options."

For the first time, she smiled. He would've missed it if he hadn't been carefully studying her face; the corners of her mouth flicked up for only a second. Aiden didn't know why that made his chest ache so fiercely. He only knew he wanted to make her smile again.

"You said in your application you want to be fixed. But fixing implies something is broken, and nothing I've seen or heard so far makes me believe that's true. Inexperience and damage are two very different things."

She opened her mouth, but then seemed to remember his earlier admonition and closed it again. Absolutely fucking perfect. Olivia appeared to be a fast learner, like all true submissives. They wanted nothing more than to please their Dominant at any cost . . . unlike the bratty pain sluts who disobeyed any time they wanted a punishment. He'd dealt with enough of those to last him a lifetime.

The next week was going to be fucking fantastic.

"You may speak."

"I just . . ." Her brows furrowed, and she chewed on her bottom lip for a moment. "You read my whole application, Sir?"

He nodded. "Of course." At least a hundred damn times.

"So you know I'm not saying I'm broken cause I haven't—cause I'm too scared to—"

"Yes, I know," he interrupted, saving her from struggling through any more of her explanation. She was blushing furiously, and clearly couldn't find the right words. "And I appreciate how honest you are. It's a rare quality, and one that shows an incredible amount of strength. As does giving me your submission. Giving yourself over to me, trusting me to give you exactly what you need, and not take things too far . . . there's nothing stronger or more beautiful in this world, as far as I'm concerned."

The lust and adoration in her eyes at that moment could've stopped a truck. *Crisis averted*. There would be no refunds issued today.

"Now," Aiden said, drawing out the word, lifting one corner of his mouth into a lazy smile. "Why don't you get out of that car so we can get your submission started properly. You have quite a few strikes against you, and I'm sure you'll feel better once you've atoned for them."

CHAPTER 4
Olivia

Ohmygod ohmygod ohmygod ohmygod!

This wasn't really happening. It couldn't be. There was no way she was about to get her first-ever spanking on the side of a public road, right in front of a security camera.

No way was she that lucky.

And from the hottest guy she'd ever seen in real life, no less. Goddamn, the way his jeans draped across his hips, and the lean muscles visible even through his black T-shirt . . . not to mention the stubble or those deliciously deep brown eyes. She could lose herself in their intensity for hours.

Jesus fuck, she was so wet, it was a wonder there wasn't a spot on the seat when she climbed out of the car.

"Turn around and bend over the seat, Olivia," Aiden ordered.

Her heart was practically thumping right out of her chest as she obeyed, putting her palms down onto the leather. His hand appeared between her shoulder blades, his skin hot against hers, applying gentle but constant pressure until she dropped down onto her elbows.

"Good girl."

God almighty, it did amazing things to her whenever he said that. It was like a secret password to make her clit throb with need.

"Now let's see. We have the tardiness, the poor language, and the lack of proper address. Anything else?"

"I interrupted you, Sir," she answered without hesitation. She didn't think she could lie to him even if she wanted to. Besides, she was already being punished anyway. In for a penny, in for a pound.

"*Very* good girl. For that, I'll let you come after your punishment."

Olivia whimpered. She couldn't help herself.

"I love this outfit," Aiden said, running one hand slowly from her hip down the outside of her thigh. "Did you wear this for me?"

"Yes, Sir." It was her favorite of the clothing she'd bought to wear to BDSM clubs, which had been gathering dust at the back of her closet until today. A black mini dress that crisscrossed over her torso—forming a deep V that displayed her breasts to great advantage, if she did say so herself—paired with sheer thigh-high stockings and kitten heels.

A fingertip traced over the lace at the top of one stocking. "Beautiful." His hand traveled higher, sliding under the dress and pushing it up over her hips. He ran both thumbs along the edges of her lace panties. "Absolutely beautiful." He started to pull her panties down, and she squirmed, unable to help herself. Immediately, his hands clamped down over her hips, digging into her skin enough to hurt. "Be still."

"Yes, Sir." She didn't move another muscle as he dragged her panties down to her upper thighs.

"You're awfully wet for a naughty girl who's about to be punished," he said, sliding one finger through her slit.

"Is—is that not allowed, Sir?" Fucking hell, had she seriously messed up already? Was she supposed to be scared, not aroused? But how was she supposed to help it?

In answer, he dipped one finger into her pussy, then used her moisture to make slow, gentle circles over her clit. "Do I seem unhappy to you?"

Moaning, she pushed back against his hand, desperate for more pressure. In an instant, his finger was gone, and she had to hold in an anguished cry.

"Don't be greedy," he scolded, but he sounded amused, not angry.

When he rested his hand against her ass, it was warm and hard and so spectacularly wonderful. Olivia felt like she'd been waiting her entire life to reach this exact moment. Like nothing that came before or after could ever compare to how she felt right now.

God, I hope that isn't true.

"Since it's your first time, I'll go a little easy on you," Aiden said, starting to rub her bottom with those same slow, gentle circles. "Do you remember the safe word you chose in your application?"

She was so distracted by the feel of his skin against hers that she was only half paying attention. "Mmm," she said noncommittally.

"Olivia." His voice was stern, and her eyes snapped open. "I asked you a question. I expect a proper answer."

Fuck. What had he said? Something about her application . . . *her safe word.* That was it.

"Orchid, Sir."

Leaning into her, he traced the orchid tattoo on her upper arm with his fingertip. "Good girl. Let's get started. Consider this your welcome to the world where you so obviously belong." He stepped away from her, exposing her bared ass to the afternoon sun.

Crack.

"Oh my fucking God." The words spilled out of Olivia's mouth quite against her will. It felt that fucking good.

A soft chuckle from Aiden. "Please try to remember one of the things you're being punished for is bad language."

"Oh. Right. Sorry, Sir."

Crack. Crack. Crack.

Those three firm swats left her breathless. This was going easy on her? She'd expected an almost playful spanking that barely even turned her skin pink. She hadn't been close to right. If this was what his hand felt like, she couldn't wait until he spanked her with other things. The Manor had to be full of paddles and floggers and straps and—

Another long volley of spanks interrupted her lewd reverie. "Fuuuu-uuuu . . ." She only managed to stop herself from finishing the word at the last second, and she let it trail off instead.

Aiden's hand rested on her bottom again. Before, it had been warm and somewhat calming. Now, the friction as his skin moved across hers made her flaming ass burn even hotter. She shivered.

"I might have to gag you in the future," he said, his chuckle low and dark. "To save you from yourself. Though I assure you, I'd be happy to prolong any punishment if that's what you truly need."

Olivia wasn't sure if he was expecting a response, and before she made up her mind, he started spanking her again. Only this time, he didn't let up after a handful of swats.

She realized she'd been subconsciously keeping count when he hit ten. She was panting and moaning like a two-penny whore by twenty-five. After that, she stopped counting and just let herself feel. Every time his hand impacted with one of her cheeks, it was like an explosion of heat and energy. And she didn't only feel it on her ass. She felt it *every-where*. It was like her entire body was charged with an electric current, all running straight to her nipples and clit and achingly empty pussy.

Then his hands moved lower, two fingers plunging into her, filling that desperate void. It felt so good, but not enough, not even remotely enough.

"Please," she said, the word slipping out before she'd even thought it. "Please, please, please, *please*." She didn't even know what she was begging for. But Aiden would know. He had to know.

With his other hand, he pinched her clit. Hard. She cried out, the whole of the English language quite forgotten at that point. And as he rubbed against the tiny bundle of nerves in faster and faster circles, his fingers still pumping in and out of her, harder and faster and unending, she mewled like a bitch in heat.

She may have screamed when the orgasm finally hit her, an explosion of pleasure unlike anything she'd ever felt before. She honestly couldn't remember.

At long last, everything was quiet and still.

Dear God in heaven. She must be dead. Either that or she was having an out-of-body experience. Those were the only possible explanations for the amazing, floaty feeling running through her entire body. She tried to move, but her limbs were full of lead. She could hardly even feel her legs.

Somewhere in the back of her mind, she knew Aiden was pulling up her panties and lowering her dress. But she couldn't summon enough mental energy to care.

Aiden leaned over her, his thighs pressing against hers, his chest hard against her back. "Let's get you to bed, beautiful girl," he whispered against her ear. Then she was rising, though she couldn't remember deciding to do so, or even how to stand at that point. Aiden was in total control, scooping her into his arms and cradling her gently against his chest.

She tried to open her eyes. To look up at him. To thank him for the glorious, earth-shattering experience he'd given her, and for taking care of her now. But it was like her eyelids were glued shut.

"I'm floating," she said, not sure why, but needing to say the words. "You made me fly."

And then she was fast asleep.

CHAPTER 5
Aiden

Zach was standing behind the reception desk when they entered the lobby, hands on his slender hips and eyebrows arched to high heaven. He was trying to look stern, but was obviously fighting back a grin.

Aiden simply dropped Olivia's car keys and cell phone on the counter and continued right on up to their room. He didn't owe anyone explanations for how he chose to do his job. And his primary concern had to be the sleeping woman in his arms.

He'd never had a sub slip so quickly or so deeply into subspace before. Not that it didn't make sense. After almost two decades of pent-up lust and sexual frustration, she'd finally gotten what her body was desperate for—and not to be too cocky, but he was one hundred percent sure that was the best orgasm of her life. He'd simply have to be careful with her in the future. Unless, of course, he wanted all their scenes to be short.

Yeah, no thanks. He had so many delectable plans for Olivia Adams. It would take months, maybe even years to run through everything he wanted to do to her body. And he only had a single week.

Aiden had never been able to resist trying to fix things that were broken. It was why he'd spent seven years after college renovating old houses, even though his parents hadn't once missed an opportunity for snide comments about wasting his degree. Not even when he wrote them a check for every penny they'd spent on his tuition, after selling his third flip for a massive profit. They were simply too proud to admit he was successful doing what they saw as *menial labor*.

Weren't too proud to cash the check, though, the assholes.

No matter what he said to them, they simply didn't get it. The work brought him a fulfillment he could only get one other way; that's why he'd known renovating the Manor and building their new business from the ground up would bring him the greatest fulfillment of all.

It was also why he'd always been the most drawn to subs with a fucked-up past.

Subs like Olivia.

He'd meant it when he told her she wasn't broken. But Christ did she need him.

Aiden laid her gently on the king-sized bed in their room, taking extra care to arrange two pillows beneath her head and smoothing back her hair. He got her heels and stockings off, but otherwise left her clothes alone. She'd be more comfortable if he got her out of that sexy getup she'd wrapped her luscious curves in, but he didn't think she was the type of woman who'd enjoy waking up naked and not knowing how she got that way.

Yes, he'd have to be very careful with Olivia.

Then again, given the way she'd reacted during their first scene, maybe he didn't need to worry after all.

It was a little over two hours before Olivia finally stirred. Aiden was beside her, propped up against the headboard with a couple of pillows, reading one of the sappy romance novels Zach left all over the house. How this one had made its way into a guest room was a mystery.

He put the book aside, not bothering to mark his place, and shifted so he was semi-hovering over her. "Welcome back," he said, voice soft, lips holding a hint of a smile.

She blinked large, sleepy blue eyes and stretched like a cat. "I can't believe I fell asleep on you. I've been so nervous about coming here, I haven't slept well the last several nights. And then you went and did *that*." Her smile was charmingly shy. "Anyway, I'm really sorry."

"Don't be." He ran a hand lazily through her long black curls. They were impossibly soft. "I take it as a compliment I made you feel that good."

A blush pinkened her cheeks, but she didn't look away. "Thank you. Not just for the . . . well, you know. But what you said to me before. I don't think I'm scared anymore."

"Well, we can't have that," Aiden joked, flipping her over onto her belly and giving her ass a couple of playful spanks. Her yelp of surprise dissolved into an adorable giggle. "You need to be scared of me at all times."

"Oh, I am, Sir. Positively terrified."

"Good girl." He slipped his hand under her dress and pushed aside her panties. She was soaking. "Wet for me already? You've been awake for, what, two minutes?"

She gave him a coy look over her shoulder. "I assumed I needed to be wet for you at all times, too, Sir."

He slid two fingers into her, and she let out a low moan. "*Very* good answer," he said, hooking his fingers to find her G-spot. She gasped when he hit it. "Good answers like that deserve a reward."

Aiden took his time with her second orgasm. The first had been fast and hard and overwhelming—exactly what she'd needed to get over her fear and start lowering her barriers. But this moment was far more intimate (and far more private, with no voyeuristic receptionists watching their every move), and he wanted to give her the worshipful attention she deserved.

When at last he'd wrung as much pleasure out of her shuddering body as it could take, he slipped his fingers into his mouth, sucking off her sweet juices. "Delicious," he said, adoring her sudden blush. "I can't wait to eat your pussy, Olivia."

Just when he thought she couldn't possibly turn a deeper shade of red.

Fighting back a laugh, he put her out of her misery. "But perhaps we should both eat something a little more substantial first. I'm sure you're hungry. Let's head downstairs before the kitchen closes for the night."

He started to stand, but turned back at her curious, "What about you?"

Ahh, music to his ears. It had been a while since he'd had a guest who cared about anything beyond her own pleasure. "What about me?"

"I've already come twice. But you haven't at all." Her gaze slid down to the obvious bulge of his erection. "Should I—"

"Dinner first," Aiden interrupted, sliding off the bed and pulling her up after him. "No, leave your shoes. We're only going downstairs. Then we'll have all night for whatever comes into my depraved little mind."

She giggled again—not a nervous, high-pitched sound, but low and throaty. He could lose himself in a laugh like that.

As he guided her to the door, Olivia took in the rich, dark wood and leather of the furniture, the thick rugs, the deep gray walls, the stone fireplace. "It's so beautiful," she said, genuine awe in her voice. "I can't believe I'm really here. I keep expecting to wake up in my apartment and realize it's all been a dream."

"Hopefully I'll be able to convince you I'm real by the end of the week," he said, resisting the urge to grin like an idiot as he opened the door for her. What was it about this woman? He couldn't remember the last time he'd been so boyishly infatuated. Probably not since college, when he'd had his very first sub, years before he and the others had banded together to open the Manor. And hadn't that been a fucking disaster.

If he was honest with himself, though, he already knew what it was. It was the raw honesty and pain that had filled her application. It had drawn him to her like a moth to a flame, exactly as Zach had known it would. The six-month span between her application and arrival had been torture.

Aiden had expected the dining room to be empty. It was almost eight o'clock, and by this time, everyone tended to be well into their planned activities for the evening. But Jonathan was seated at the head of the antique table, the tall, willowy blonde perched on his lap taking tiny bites from his fork. She looked familiar. Definitely a repeat guest, though he couldn't remember a name.

Jonathan and his sub looked up when they entered the room. The former gave Olivia a once-over and a polite nod, while the latter's gaze fixed on Aiden and never left. Her eyes narrowed ever so slightly.

Interesting.

"Won't you join us for dinner?" Jonathan said, sweeping a hand toward the high-backed chair to his right. The way they were sitting, he didn't have a good view of his sub's face, and didn't seem to realize anything was amiss.

Olivia sure did, though. Aiden's hand was on her lower back, and he'd felt her stiffen.

The blonde's gaze stayed glued to him as they made their way to the table. It was practically burning his skin. Damnit, he wished he could remember who she was. He'd clearly done something to piss her off.

Aiden dropped into his chair, then hauled Olivia onto his lap when she started to pull out the seat next to his. She made a surprised little squeak and blushed furiously, hiding a smile. Pleased with her reaction, he wrapped one arm around her, letting his hand rest on her thigh.

"Olivia, this is Jonathan Hale," Aiden said, nodding toward his sort-of boss. Each of the Doms in residence more or less did their own thing, but Fairford Manor had all been Jonathan's idea, and he'd invested by far the most money into buying the property and renovating the house. He'd taken on the role as de facto leader from the start, and the rest of them had never questioned it.

"Very pleased to meet you, Sir," Olivia said, giving him a shy smile.

Returning the smile, Jonathan said, "I hope you're enjoying your stay at the Manor so far."

She took in the damask wallpaper, ornate brass chandelier, and gleaming mahogany furniture with an expression of joy, exactly as she'd done in their suite. "It's beautiful. I don't think I've ever seen somewhere more beautiful in my life."

Aiden's chest swelled with pride.

Jonathan gave her an approving look. "What a sweet little sub you have, Aiden," he said, voice warm. His own sub visibly stiffened, throwing a jealous glare at Olivia. "And let me introduce—"

"Oh, you don't need to introduce me," the blonde interrupted. "Aiden and I already know each other, don't we, Sir?"

He may not have recognized her face, but Christ almighty, he remembered that grating voice. It was Stacey Blackwood—the not-really-a-sub socialite he'd been so relieved to rid himself of. "It's nice to see you again, Stacey," he lied.

"Isn't it? Though I must say, I'm surprised to see you," she said, her smile as fake as her hair color. "I naturally thought you must have left."

He arranged his features into a blandly polite expression. "I'm not sure what you mean."

"Well, when I was assigned a different Dom, I naturally assumed you were no longer employed here." Because Stacey Blackwood was never ever denied something she wanted. *Naturally.*

Aiden only resisted the urge to roll his eyes for Jonathan's sake. She'd applied for another stay within a few months of her last one, specifically requesting Aiden as her host again. He'd begged one of the others to take her instead, not sure he could survive another week with the woman. Jonathan had drawn the short straw.

"I hope you're not complaining," Jonathan said, a hint of a warning in his voice.

"Of *course* not, Sir," Stacey said, twisting around in his lap and blinking up at him with big doe eyes. "Forgive my rudeness. I couldn't be happier to be chosen by the head Dom himself. It's an *honor* to serve you."

Her simpering voice made Aiden want to gag. How had he put up with her bullshit act for a whole week? If he had to guess, there wasn't a single truly submissive bone in her body.

Jonathan had clearly come to the same conclusion. He met Stacey's gaze with a stony one of his own, then returned to their meal without a word. Aiden knew from experience Jonathan had a long-ass week ahead of him. He would've felt bad if he wasn't so relieved it wasn't him.

Before the silence could become too awkward, the door between the dining room and the kitchen swung open. The Manor's private chef, Gabriel, bustled in with a dinner tray.

"Bonsoir monsieur, mademoiselle!" he said in the ridiculous fake French accent he liked to use around guests. ("It adds a touch of class to the place!" he insisted any time one of the partners had asked him to knock it off.) "Tonight, we have freshly made linguine pasta in a creamy white wine sauce, with Mediterranean *palourdes*—"

"That means clams," Aiden whispered in her ear, and she laughed.

"—and wilted spinach," Gabriel finished, raising his voice slightly and giving Aiden a stern look. He placed a large bowl with enough pasta for two on the table in front of them, then added silverware and a wine glass. "I've paired your dinner this evening with a lovely 2002 Muscadet, which perfectly complements the briny flavor of the clams." He poured a heathy portion of the white wine into the glass, then left the bottle within easy reach. "*Bon appétit!*"

"*Merci!*" Olivia said as the chef hurried from the room, clearly not suspecting he was actually from Wisconsin. She leaned over the bowl, breathing deeply. "Oh my God, this smells *amazing*."

"The food here always is," Stacey said in that sickly sweet voice of hers. She smirked. "Be careful, though . . . you don't want to eat too many carbs. Aiden's got to be struggling to hold you on his lap as it is."

"That's enough," Jonathan said, as Aiden opened his mouth to say something quite a bit harsher. "I think we're done here. Aiden, Olivia, please enjoy your dinner." Then he stood and marched Stacey from the room, a hand firmly clamped around her upper arm.

"If he's smart, he'll gag her for the rest of her stay," Aiden muttered, trying to rein in his temper. He couldn't wait to say *I told you so* the next time he and Jonathan were alone. "I don't want you to listen to a word she said, understand?"

"Yes, Sir," she answered, but all the excitement had left her voice. Christ, he hoped Jonathan was painting that jealous bitch's ass red already.

Aiden grabbed her hips and easily lifted her, turning her in his lap so he could look into her eyes. "I mean it, Olivia," he said, softening his voice. "She's bitter, because she knows I didn't want to see her again, and she can see how crazy I am about you."

That got her to smile, just a little bit. "You're crazy about me?" she asked with a flirty lilt to her voice.

"Isn't it obvious?" he asked, leaning in for a slow kiss. She melted against his body, arching her back and neck as he deepened the kiss, tasting her, claiming her. When at last he pulled away, she was breathing heavily, her eyes still closed. He gave each eyelid a gentle kiss. "Now let's eat this delicious meal before Gabriel gets mad at us for letting it go cold, and yells a bunch of what may or may not be real French—"

"I heard that!" Gabriel called from the kitchen, making Olivia laugh.

"—and then the real fun can start."

CHAPTER 6
Olivia

O livia expected to return to their suite after dinner, but instead, he led her past the staircase and deeper into the house. "Where are we going, Sir?" she asked, a little disappointed. Hadn't he said they were going to have fun after dinner? She'd assumed that meant sex.

"You'll find out shortly," he promised, the hand on the small of her back propelling her down a long hallway. They passed a study with floor-to-ceiling bookshelves, a game room with a gorgeous old pool table and several card tables, and some sort of formal parlor with antique furniture upholstered in blue velvet. Every single room was empty.

Olivia resisted the urge to sulk. Apparently everyone else was off having sex, so what was Aiden stalling for?

That stupid cow Stacey had been trying to break her down so she'd feel better about herself. She'd dealt with plenty of small, petty people exactly like her in her lifetime. But what if Aiden *did* think her ass was a little too big, her thighs a little too wide? Olivia had always been super curvy, though it had mostly stopped bothering her sometime during college, after she'd left home for good. If Aiden didn't want to fuck her, though . . .

The next door they came to was closed, with an electric keypad above the handle. Aiden punched in a six-digit code, and the door unlocked with a little click. He pulled it open to reveal a dimly lit staircase. Sensual music with a baseline she felt in her belly drifted up from below.

Okay, maybe she'd jumped to the wrong conclusion. Sexy times were clearly a go.

Without a word, Aiden led her down the wide staircase, and she was so revved up she fought the urge to fidget. She'd never been in a real, live dungeon before. She only hoped it lived up to her imagination.

When they reached the bottom, she couldn't help but gasp. The dungeon was *enormous*. It had to run the whole length of the house, and was appointed with pretty much every kinky implement and piece of equipment she'd ever seen online or read about in a book. With the low lighting, the music, and the dark gray of the walls, it was like walking into her sexiest, dirtiest dreams.

No wonder the women who came here always raved about it being the best week of their lives.

There were four people already in the room—two other Doms and their subs, deep into scenes. Jonathan and Stacey were, thankfully, nowhere to be seen. He must've decided to keep her punishment a private affair.

The Manor Doms she hadn't yet met were named Mason St. John, Camden Reid, and Rafe Erikson, though she had no idea which two these were. She'd read all about them in the r/SordidFairfordAffairs subreddit, but she'd never seen any pictures. Not surprising, with no phones or recording devices allowed on property. Some of the other women complained about all the secrecy, but Olivia thought it added an exciting layer of mystery.

There was a tall, lean Dom in slacks and a white button-up, the sleeves rolled to reveal the hard muscles of his forearms. His sub was cuffed to a chain that dangled from the ceiling, and moaned nonstop as he fucked her fast and hard from behind. His hand was wrapped tightly in her long, red hair, and a black leather riding crop was abandoned on the floor beside them.

The Dom built like a football player and wearing nothing but black leather pants had his sub bound to a Saint Andrew's cross, and was making evenly spaced stripes across her ass and upper thighs with a rattan cane. Each time the cane fell, she let out a sob, and then called out a number. She was already up to nineteen. God almighty, that was a hell of a lot of strokes. All Olivia's reading and research said nothing in the dungeon hurt as much as a cane; that woman must have a fuckton of experience, or else be a *major* pain slut.

Olivia had never been so turned on in her entire life. She was practically drooling.

"You like to watch and be watched, don't you?" Aiden said, his breath hot against her ear.

She shivered. "Yes, Sir." It had been a fantasy of hers for most of her adult life, though she'd never found someone who could make it a reality before today.

He trailed a line of soft kisses up her neck and around the shell of her ear. "I thought so. When I showed you the security camera this afternoon, your pupils dilated, and your breath quickened. You were excited someone might be watching your spanking, weren't you?"

Her heart was racing, her clit already throbbing. "Yes, Sir."

"What if someone had driven by?" he teased, moving behind her and holding her against his chest. "What if some stranger had seen your bare ass on display, getting the punishment you so rightly deserved?"

"Oh, God." The words came out in a breathy rush, and she closed her eyes, imagining the scene he was describing. What if the person had stopped and demanded to know what was going on? Would she have been mortified?

Or excited?

"You're having all sorts of naughty thoughts now, aren't you?" He sounded positively delighted at the prospect.

She nodded, not trusting her voice anymore. She was so turned on she could barely breathe.

"Care to see what happens to naughty little girls with filthy minds in a place like this?"

It was a good thing he was holding onto her, because she was weak in the knees. "*Please.*"

With a dark chuckle, Aiden led her deeper into the dungeon. Olivia studied the various pieces of kinky furniture and equipment as they wove through the room, wondering which ones she'd try out during her stay. There was one versatile looking table with D-Rings evenly spaced all the way around the edge, a variety of restraints stored underneath, that particularly piqued her curiosity.

When Aiden finally stopped, they were in front of a black metal spanking bench with leather padding. Thick leather straps with large silver buckles dangled from the various platforms.

"Strip," Aiden ordered, his gaze sweeping the length of her. "It's time for me to see the rest of this luscious body. I've been more than patient."

Olivia felt like she'd been doused with a bucket of freezing water.

It wasn't that she was afraid of being naked. She'd stopped being shy about her body around the same time she hit thirty. They say with age comes wisdom, but in her opinion, with age comes indifference. She simply didn't care about shit like that anymore.

But he'd asked her to strip. Was he being literal? She had no idea how to do a sexy striptease. She'd probably look like a complete moron if she even tried. Or was she overthinking it? Maybe she should undress like she would any other time, and all he cared about was the naked part. Or would he be pissed off she wasn't being all hot and seductive like all his previous subs had surely been?

"I don't like having to repeat myself," Aiden said, a hard edge entering his voice.

Oh, fuckity fuck fuck fuck, why was her brain like this? All she had to do was take off her goddamn clothes. She'd done that a million times in her life. Why was she always making a big deal out of nothing?

Clearly, her fears about fucking everything up if she went to a dungeon alone had been quite well-founded. Aaaaand now she was starting to hyperventilate. God and hell, she wanted to die.

"Shh," Aiden soothed, pulling her against his chest. He gently rubbed her back with one hand and buried the other in her hair. "It's all right. Tell me what's wrong."

Fuck, he smelled so good, like mountain air and woodsmoke, lemongrass and leather. It was intoxicating. And the feel of his muscles through his shirt made her want to run her hands all over them. Only she could be in the most amazing dungeon ever, with the tastiest morsel of a man who ever existed, and ruin *everything* by fucking crying.

Aiden waited patiently for her to get her shit together. "I'm sorry," she whispered at last.

"Don't be sorry," he said. "You've done nothing wrong. Just tell me what happened."

Olivia was grateful her face was still pressed against his chest, so she didn't have to look him in the eye. "I'm so stupid."

He scoffed. "You're an accountant. I feel quite confident you're not stupid. Now keep talking."

"Well," she said, drawing out the word, giving her a few seconds to think. "Remember what I said in my application? How I've known I was submissive since I was seventeen, but I was always too afraid to actually do anything about it?"

Aiden went very still. It was several tense moments before he said, "Are you saying you don't wish to continue?"

"*No!*" she practically shouted, pushing away from his chest, looking up at him with pleading eyes. "Please, that's not it at all. I don't want to stop. Don't send me away."

He cupped her face in both hands. "No one's sending you anywhere. Please explain what you were saying."

"You said strip, and I didn't know if you meant just take my clothes off, or like make it sexy, or what. And it's like I wrote in my application, I know there must be a million and one rules about these kinds of things, but how am I supposed to know them all? I've never done any of this before. What if I mess up, and you think I'm stupid, and you don't want to scene with me anymore, and—"

Aiden silenced her with a finger over her lips. "Breathe." He waited until she'd taken several deep breaths before continuing. "I understand. And I'm sorry. I knew that, and I should've taken it into account before I spoke."

"No, it's not your fault," she hurried to say. "It's me who's—"

"I'm your Dom," he interrupted, and his tone allowed for no further argument. "It's my job to know exactly what you need and make sure you get it. I give you my word, I'll do everything I can to keep this from happening again."

His words filled her chest with warmth. No one she'd ever met in her life had made her feel so safe, so protected. So *worthy* of protection.

"Now." Aiden gave her a soft, sensuous kiss. "Let's try this again, shall we? Turn around."

Grateful for the easy order, she did as she was told.

"Your skin is so soft," he said, running his fingertips down the middle of her back, between her shoulder blades. "I love touching you."

She sighed contentedly as he slowly unzipped her dress. Next, he gently ran his fingers along the tops of her shoulders, pushing her straps down her arms until the dress fell to her waist.

"Oh, I love this." He walked around in front of her, staring unashamedly at her breasts. He ran one finger along the top of her demi bra, then brushed his thumbs over her nipples, which hardened at the touch. "I must admit, I have a thing for black lace." He pushed her dress over her hips, letting it pool at her feet, and looked his fill at her matching lingerie. "Do you have any idea how beautiful you are?"

At that moment, she did. Olivia felt more beautiful than she ever had in her life.

Unhooking her bra, Aiden pulled it quickly down her arms and tossed it aside. A few seconds later, her panties were down around her ankles. His fingers found her nipples again, rolling and pulling, hard enough to send a line of pleasure straight to her clit. She wouldn't have been surprised if she was dripping down her thighs.

"Come," he said, taking her hand, helping her step out of her clothes.

She followed him the rest of the way to the spanking bench without hesitation. He knew exactly what she needed and how to give it to her. She'd finally found her Dom.

"Knees here and here," Aiden said, pointing at the padded platforms for her legs. After she knelt down, he gently pushed her forward until her stomach and breasts were pressed against the larger platform for her torso. He guided her arms into the position he wanted with a firm grip. "I'm going to restrain you now."

The leather straps were cold against her skin, and she shivered as he buckled the first two, one around her waist and the other below her shoulder blades. More straps went around her wrists and forearms, ankles and calves. She tried to wriggle around a little bit, but he had her strapped in good and tight.

Aiden leaned down and planted a kiss on the soft spot behind her ear. "Be a good girl and be still while I go get some toys for us to play with."

"Yes, Sir," she said, her voice shaking with lust and anticipation. She couldn't see where he went, and though she wanted to crane her neck and try to find him, she did as she was told. Anything to be his good girl.

The song changed, and she closed her eyes, letting the new bass beat roll through her. She didn't want to overthink things anymore. She only wanted to feel whatever Aiden wanted her to feel, and make him proud.

When Aiden returned, he walked in front of her, showing her the items he'd chosen. In one hand was a wooden paddle, it's circular end about five inches across. In the other, he held a sizable black metal anal plug, with a large blue jewel on the base.

"Look at me, Olivia." She did as she was told. "I need to know if you were telling the truth in your application."

"What do you mean, Sir?"

He held up the plug. "You wrote that you have several butt plugs at home. That you enjoy the feeling of having your ass filled when you come, and nearly all your fantasies include anal sex. I need to know if that's true, or if you were saying what you thought we'd want to hear. Because if you're an anal novice, this is going to be way too big for you."

She took another look at the large plug, and her heart skipped a beat in the best possible way. Oh, fuck yeah, this was going to be a fun night. "Everything in my application was true, Sir. I promise."

Aiden's answering grin sent a wave of pride through Olivia. Knowing she was exactly what he wanted was such a heady feeling.

"You also said you've always wanted to be paddled. But if this is too much for you"—he rotated the paddle in his hand, showing her the intricate floral pattern engraved on the other side—"we have about a hundred other paddles in this place, and I can choose a less severe one. What's your safe word?"

"Orchid, Sir."

"Good girl." His fingertips found the ink on her right arm again—an intricate monochrome orchid. "Did you choose that as your safe word because of your tattoo?"

She closed her eyes, relishing the goosebumps erupting across her skin at his touch. "It's my favorite flower, Sir."

He traced his fingers up her arm, brushing softly along her shoulder and neck, until finally grazing his thumb over her lips. "Don't be afraid to use it. I give you my word I won't be angry or disappointed if you do. This is about giving you what you need. If I'm not doing that, using your safe word is the only way to let me know. Otherwise, no matter what you say, even if you plead and beg, we keep going. Do you understand?"

God, he was so fucking perfect. He'd obviously meant it when he promised to guide her through every step, and make sure she didn't have further cause to panic. "Yes, Sir. I understand."

Aiden walked to the back of the bench, trailing his hand along her side as he did so, making goosebumps rise all over her body. "You have the most incredible ass, Olivia." He cupped one cheek with his large hand, squeezing hard. "So spankable." His hand moved toward the center, and a single finger circled her rear hole, pressing in the tiniest bit. "So fuckable."

She moaned, wishing she wasn't restrained. That she could push back against his hand, taking more of his finger into her.

There was the sound of a bottle opening, and then something cool and wet drizzled into the crack of her ass. Aiden gathered the lube on his fingers, coating them generously, and then plunged a finger into her asshole. He pumped it in and out a few times, spreading the lube around, preparing her for the plug.

Olivia had done this to herself more times than she could count. She loved to have a plug in while she read her sexy books, and especially when giving herself pleasure. A couple of times, she'd even worn one as she cleaned her apartment, pretending her imaginary Dom had ordered her to do so as punishment for some misdeed or other.

But that was nothing at all like what Aiden was doing to her now. How he was making her feel. She wished her legs weren't restrained so far apart. She was desperate to clench her thighs together, to try to relieve some of the ache.

A few seconds after Aiden removed his finger, the blunt tip of the anal plug pressed against her tight ring of muscle. He pushed it into her, taking his sweet time like an absolute devil. When the thickest part of the plug was finally in her, she let out a long, low moan of relief, but then he pulled it out, making her groan. He pumped the plug in and out of her ass several more times, until she was both moaning with desire and ready to scream in frustration.

"My, my," Aiden said with a dark chuckle. "We are a little anal slut, aren't we?"

He had no fucking idea.

When at last the plug was fully seated, the wide base cold against her spread cheeks, she let out a long, shuddering breath. How she'd survived her entire adult life without experiencing anything like this was beyond her. What an empty, boring life it had been.

Before she'd even started adjusting to the sheer size of the plug, Aiden rubbed the smooth side of the paddle against her bottom, letting her feel the warm, lacquered wood. "Six months you made me wait for you," he said, resting a hand on her lower back. "Six months, when I had openings starting in March. Do you know how hard it's been? How I've longed for you?"

Was that true? Had he really longed for her, the way she'd longed for him? It was almost too good to believe. "I—I'm really sorry, Sir. I didn't know."

The paddle continued its slow slide across her skin, back and forth, back and forth. "Why did you make me wait, Olivia? Why did you torture us both?"

Guilt formed a deep, aching pit in her stomach, and she blinked back tears. "I was excited to come here, but also so afraid. I—I thought it would give me enough time to get used to the idea." And yet she'd still had two panic attacks on day one. If anything, all the buildup had made it even more terrifying.

That had clearly been a great fucking plan.

"I see." The smooth wood stilled, pressed firmly against the center of her ass. "And now that you're here, you want to be my good girl, and make it up to me, don't you?"

She very nearly said, *Fuck yes*, but stopped herself at the last second. The whole no cursing thing was taking some getting used to. "Yes, Sir. More than anything."

Aiden's hand brushed down her spine, coming to a rest at the small of her back. "I think we're going to start with six strokes with the paddle. Let's see how you take those, and I'll decide where to go from there."

Six didn't seem too bad. Quite tame, actually—almost a letdown. The women in her books could all take way more than that. And the sub across the dungeon had received twenty-five with the much more severe cane. She tried to keep her butt relaxed as Aiden raised the paddle for the first stroke.

Fucking God and holy fucking Jesus, that hurt. How she managed to keep that string of profane blasphemy from coming out of her mouth, she had no idea. But that's what Aiden wanted, so the only sound she made was a high, keening cry.

"That's for January," Aiden said, rubbing the paddle over her bottom to relieve some of the sting.

Another stroke, even harder than the first one.

"February."

They ran through the six months of their mutual torment, her tears hot against her cheeks. For June—the hardest stroke of all—he switched to the other side of the paddle. Even though the edges were rounded and smooth, the engraving still bit into her skin, and she was sure it had left its mark.

"Beautiful," Aiden said, tracing the floral pattern on her red, swollen flesh. "You did so well."

Olivia let out a long, soft sigh. "Thank you, Sir. Thank you so much." She wasn't even sure what she was thanking him for. Calling her beautiful? Praising how she took his punishment?

Making one of her oldest, deepest fantasies a reality?

All of the above, she supposed.

There was the tear of a foil condom wrapper, and not long after, he gripped her hips. "I'm going to fuck you now, Olivia. You have permission to come."

And then he was finally inside her, pushing his whole length in with one fluid stroke. "*Holy fuck.*" The strangled words left her mouth before she could stop them. She was so impossibly full.

"Careful," Aiden warned, stopping with his cock still filling her, his hips pressed tightly against her throbbing, plugged ass. "Or I'll have to give you a few more with the paddle when we're done."

"I'm sorry, Sir," she forced out, but she wasn't really. How could he expect anything different after what he'd done to her?

Aiden's hands tightened on her hips. "See that it doesn't happen again."

After that, he began fucking her in earnest—long, hard strokes ending with the slap of skin against skin. Nothing had ever stretched and filled her like this. Never had she felt so completely controlled and owned. When Aiden switched up his angle so he hit her G-spot, God almighty, the moans that came out of her were straight-up animalistic.

"Come for me," Aiden ordered, reaching around to press one finger firmly against her clit.

She screamed as she shattered from the inside out, pleasure slamming through her like tidal waves. They rocked through her whole body, setting all her nerve endings on fire, taking every single thought from her mind except one.

How in the fuck was she going to return to her old life after this?

CHAPTER 7
Aiden

"Please don't think I'm complaining," Olivia said as they ate breakfast in bed the next morning. Aiden had brought up a breakfast tray while she slept, and had lingered over feeding his still-naked sub bits of fruit and pancakes for the last fifteen minutes. "Far from it. And not that I think it should be! But isn't prostitution, like . . ." She blushed from the base of her throat all the way to the tips of her ears. It was absolutely fucking adorable. "Illegal?"

Aiden tried to keep a straight face. He really did. But he only lasted about two and a half seconds before he threw back his head and laughed. "I can't *believe* you just called me a prostitute."

That glorious blush he loved so much deepened a good three shades. "I didn't mean—I mean, I did, but it wasn't supposed to be a *bad* thing! I only—"

He silenced her rambling with a kiss. She tried to pull away at first, still attempting to explain, but he wrapped an arm around her, holding her close until she melted against him. When at last they separated, lust had replaced the worry and fear in her eyes.

"Our guests pay to stay at a beautiful, high-end resort with large suites, a heated pool, exquisite mountain views, miles of hiking trails, and five-star dining," he said, keeping his voice smooth and even so she wouldn't think he was laughing at her again. "What consenting adults choose to do while they're here is no one's business but their own."

One corner of Olivia's mouth twisted up into a wry smile. "Your entire basement is one big BDSM dungeon. Whatever could people be planning to do when they come here?"

"Don't get sarcastic with me, little girl," Aiden said, giving her bottom a firm swat. But he knew she wouldn't take him seriously. He was smiling when he said it. "And if you follow that same line of thinking, why else would people go to a BDSM club? If you went to a club, and scened with someone who worked there, would that make him a prostitute?"

That finally convinced her. "No, I guess not," she said, heaving a dramatic sigh. "Oh, well. I was all excited. My friend Jen is always trying to get me to have more sex. I was gonna tell her I hired a gigolo to shut her up."

He laughed again. Christ, he couldn't remember the last time a guest had made him truly laugh. "I mean, gigolo has a nice ring to it. As long as you promise to keep it classy, I guess I don't mind. I can't have people thinking I'm some common streetwalker."

"Hey, now!" she said, barely holding in her own laughter. "Common streetwalkers have feelings, too! Haven't you ever seen *Pretty Woman*?"

"I refuse to be compared to that movie unless you're taking me to the opera in a private jet." He pretended to think about it for a moment. "Though admittedly, I don't think I could pull off that red dress."

Olivia dissolved into a fit of giggles, which he helped along by tickling her sides. Had he really only known her for less than a full day? That didn't seem possible. It felt like he'd known her for months already.

Though hadn't he, in a way? He'd read her application so many times in the last six months, memorizing all those shards of her soul she'd chosen to bare on its pages. He knew the *real* Olivia. The one she was too afraid to let the rest of the world see.

Phrases from her application ran through his mind, like the crawl of a news ticker.

How can I be expected to trust a perfect stranger, when people who were supposed to love me cut me so deeply?

I've made my life as calm and organized and secure as I can. I finally feel safe. But I'm bored out of my fucking mind.

And, of course, I want to give myself to someone who I'll know, beyond a shadow of a doubt, can give me the pain my body needs, without putting more scars on my soul. I think it's the only way to fix me.

He'd learned last night she was drunk when she wrote the application. Not surprising, really. That kind of raw honesty usually took a little liquid courage, and her vulnerability had enticed him in a way nothing else had in his thirty-five years.

"Are there really hiking trails?" Olivia asked, pulling him out of his thoughts like a hook yanking a performer offstage in an old cartoon.

It took a second for him to even register what she'd said. "That's your key takeaway from all of that?" he asked, chuckling.

Rolling her eyes, she said, "Well, it's not like you have a website where I can read about all the amenities. All the girls on Reddit talk about is sex, sex, sex."

"Mmm," he said, leaning down, catching her nipple in his mouth. He gave it a long, none-too-gentle suck. "Sex sounds fun." He rolled his tongue around the stiff bud, then pinched her other nipple between his fingers, making her gasp. "Unfortunately, I foolishly fed you all the food, and now I'm too hungry for such trivial things."

He licked a slow path between her breasts, then down her quivering belly.

"Please, Sir," she begged, her hands moving to his hair.

"Hands on the headboard," he ordered. "And don't move them until I tell you, or everything stops."

She did as she was told, flattening her palms against the smooth wood. Her eyes were screwed shut, and every muscle in her body was taut. Christ, she was sexy.

"Now be a good girl, and let me enjoy my breakfast," he said, hooking her knees over his shoulders and diving in.

She was every bit as sweet as he remembered. He devoured her like a man starved, licking her from cunt to clit, every one of her gasps and moans feeling like a fist around his cock. It didn't take long for his expert ministrations to draw the first orgasm out of her. She lifted her hips clear off the bed as she screamed her pleasure, but good little submissive that she was, her palms stayed planted against the headboard. That deserved another reward.

Aiden concentrated only on her clit the second time, applying firm pressure with his tongue, then sucking on the tiny bundle of nerves as she writhed. Her second explosion took even less time than the first, and she was still shouting, "Oh my God!" over and over when he knelt up between her thighs and took his cock in his hand.

He was pumping furiously when Olivia opened her eyes, and her heavy-lidded lust almost made him come then and there. "*Please,*" she said, wrapping her legs around him and hooking her ankles behind his thighs. "Mark me, Sir. Make me yours."

Aiden couldn't have stopped himself from coming then if he'd tried. Thick jets of his come hit her stomach as she watched, and he didn't stop until he'd milked himself of every last drop.

Collapsing onto the bed beside her, he rubbed his semen into her belly and breasts, wanting his scent to seep into her skin and never leave her. "*Mine.*"

"We're seriously doing this," Aiden said, half amused, half dumbfounded as he followed Olivia down one of the Manor's seldom used hiking trails.

She threw a flirty look over her shoulder. "Yes, we're seriously doing this. Zach said this trail leads to an overlook where you can see for hundreds of miles. I want to see it."

Fucking Zach. Aiden had given Olivia a bath after breakfast, washing her skin with gentle care, letting her soak long enough in the hot water to soothe any aches and pains from last night. He'd expected her to relax on the couch while he showered, but she'd slipped out and asked the ever so helpful receptionist about the trails Aiden now regretted mentioning.

He would've thought the man would do him a solid after Aiden got him a raise, and convinced his delectable sub to stay inside instead.

Apparently not.

The only upside was what she wore: super-tight workout pants and a sports bra. And those pants didn't leave much to the imagination; there was no doubt in his mind she wasn't wearing any panties. If he had to go hiking instead of finding new and creative ways to make her take the Lord's name in vain, at least he got to enjoy the view.

He'd also slipped a small bottle of lube into his pocket on their way out, just in case. He still hadn't fucked that fabulous ass of hers, and anything could happen in the woods.

"Oh, look!" Olivia said, bending over at the waist to examine something a few feet from the trail.

He was looking all right, though it wasn't at whatever had caught her eye. Moving up behind her, he ran his hand down the crack of her ass, cupping her pussy through the stretchy fabric.

"Aiden!" she scolded, straightening and giving his chest a playful shove.

He didn't usually let his guests call him by his name, even outside of scenes. But something about the sound of it in her sweet, playful voice stopped him from scolding her. Maybe it would be okay, so long as she remembered her place when it counted.

"Okay, okay," he said, holding his hands up in surrender. "What did you find?"

Olivia pointed down at a rotting tree stump and grinned at him. "Aren't they pretty?"

"Mushrooms," he said, voice inflectionless, face blank. "I'm looking at mushrooms."

"*Pretty* mushrooms," she insisted. "Look at the colors! Ugh, I wish I had my camera. I get why I'm not allowed to have my phone, but still."

He gave the fungus in question a closer look, willing to try since it obviously made her so happy. Large, fan-shaped growths sprouted from the dead wood, in alternating stripes of deep orange and bright yellow. He supposed the colors were quite beautiful, particularly in a forest that was otherwise mostly brown and green.

"I *might* be able to help you with that," Aiden said, opening the camera app on his cell. "The no-phone rule only applies to guests."

She eyed the phone for a moment, then smiled up at him. "Might?"

"If you're a very good girl, and show me how much you would appreciate such an enormous favor."

Olivia blushed furiously, but there was definitely a smile playing at her lips as she dropped to the forest floor. Christ, she was gorgeous on her knees. More of his plans needed to involve her kneeling before him, because his cock was straining against his pants at the sight of it.

"I'm not very good at this," she said timidly, as she fumbled with the button and fly of his jeans. "Or at least that's what my ex always said."

Aiden wanted to find out who that guy was and punch him in the mouth. The last thing Olivia needed was *more* to be anxious about. "Guy sounds like an asshole," he said, then drew in a sharp breath as she took his length in her warm hands.

That made Olivia smile. "He certainly was." She ran her thumb along the underside of his cock with enough pressure to make him suck in another harsh breath, and then looked up at him with those bright blue eyes. "Tell me what to do?"

Aiden traced a finger over the seam of her lips, parting them. "Open for me, beautiful."

Most of the tension went out of her shoulders as soon as he took control. His sweet, submissive girl.

"Start with your tongue."

She followed his instruction eagerly, running her tongue down the length of him over and over, then swirling it around the head. It felt fucking fantastic.

"Good girl," Aiden said. "Now take me into your mouth."

She was back to being hesitant, taking only the head at first, sucking on it hard enough to hollow out her cheeks. When she tried to take him deeper, she second-guessed herself and pulled away, letting his cock fall from between her lips. "Fuck," she said under her breath. Her gaze flew up to his, eyes wide. "I mean—"

"Naughty girl," Aiden scolded, though he kept his tone soft. He wasn't angry, and the last thing he wanted was to send her into another panic spiral. Clearly, she needed him to be in total control for this.

"Looks like I'm going to have to teach that dirty mouth of yours a lesson."

Taking careful hold of her face, he thrust his cock shallowly into her mouth. Once again, her whole body relaxed, and she put obvious effort into making herself his perfect little fucktoy: rounding her lips, shielding her teeth, and servicing him with more of that glorious suction.

Aiden told himself he could control his baser urges for her. He could be gentle and reintroduce her to the marvelous world of fellatio in a way that left her exhilarated, not afraid or ashamed.

But Jesus fucking Christ, she felt so goddamn good.

In the end, he lost his tenuous grasp on control. Grabbing her by the hair, he held her head in place as he pumped in and out of her mouth, bumping against the back of her throat and making her gag.

Glorious creature that she was, she didn't once try to stop him or pull away. Her eyes fluttered closed after a handful of thrusts, and she made soft, sweet little moans. Being used by him so roughly was clearly turning her on. Each sound she made vibrated through his cock, which only pushed him closer to the edge.

"Fuck, fuck, fuck, fuck, fuck, fuuuu—" His final word broke off as he came, spilling into her mouth and throat. He held her perfectly still until the last spasms ran through him. When he at last pulled out of her mouth, some of his come dripped over her lip and down her chin.

Before he could react, Olivia's tongue darted out, licking up most of his seed. What she couldn't reach with her tongue, she swiped up with a finger, popping the digit into her mouth and sucking it dry.

"Christ," he said, breathless, mesmerized. Sometimes she seemed so innocent and inexperienced, and then she went and did things like *that*. Aiden got himself resituated and closed his jeans, then handed her the phone. "For that, you can take whatever pictures you want."

Grinning like a kid at Disney World, she squatted down and snapped several photos at various angles. Then, before he even knew what was happening, she stood and snuggled into his side, holding out the phone to take a selfie. He looked like a deer in headlights in the first photo, but he recovered quickly enough. Wrapping an arm around her shoulders, he smiled for selfie number two.

"I love it," she said happily, pocketing his phone.

So did he, which was the weird part. He'd taken his fair share of photos in the bedroom or dungeon—plenty of his guests were turned on by being being filmed or photographed—but this might be the first "normal" picture he'd ever taken with a woman.

He would've gladly done so with Giselle, his first sub, but the few times he'd tried to steer them in the direction of a real relationship, she'd immediately guided things back into the sexual realm. His fourth and final attempt had involved dinner at the fanciest restaurant he could afford, cheap champagne under the stars, and a declaration of love.

Giselle had laughed in his face and ended everything, her slights to his upbringing, his social standing, and his manhood so abasing, he'd been careful never to make the same mistake again.

So why was he fighting the urge to fish his phone out of her pocket and look at the picture again?

Time for a subject change, stat.

"You know," he said, giving her a little nudge to get them moving again, "I don't remember reading 'nature lover and fungi enthusiast' on your application."

"I should think not," she teased back. "Usually when fungus comes up in the bedroom, it's not a good thing."

They laughed together as they continued down the trail, swapping jokes and taunts, and stopping often for Olivia to take pictures of whatever leaf or flower or other random thing caught her fancy. He didn't even mind all the interruptions. He loved the joy and concentration on her face as she strove to get her perfect shot.

Luckily, the overlook was only a little over a mile and a half from the Manor, and the trail wasn't even particularly steep. They probably could've made it in about thirty minutes if they hadn't taken so many little breaks. And since he'd been grinning for so long his face literally hurt, perhaps Zach hadn't fucked him over after all.

"Wow," he couldn't help saying as they went around a bend in the trees, and the overlook came into view.

"Holy crap!" Olivia said at the same time, bounding off toward the bluff. "Man, Zach wasn't kidding! This is amazing!"

Aiden followed at a more sedate pace, taking in the incredible vista.

The Green Mountains spread out before them, living up to their namesake in the early summer weather. And there wasn't a cloud in the sky, making it possible to see for the hundreds of miles Zach had promised.

"How is it possible I've lived here for six years, but never once seen this?"

She glanced at him over her shoulder, her brows slightly raised. "Do you actually live at the Manor all the time? I didn't realize."

"Not anymore," he said, moving up beside her, brushing his fingers against hers. "I have a cabin now." The other owners had procured their own little hideaways shortly after closing the deal on the mansion, but Aiden hadn't been able to afford it. Four years after the Manor had opened, though, he'd jumped a few tax brackets.

"Where is it?" Olivia asked, linking her fingers with his.

"An hour north of here. That's where I live when I'm not working. Whenever I need some time alone." Not even the other guys had been to his cabin before. He liked that it was something separate from the bustle of the resort—something completely his own.

Fairford Manor was every bit as isolated as you could want your BDSM resort to be, which wasn't too hard to achieve in northern Vermont. Yet it didn't always feel that way with so many people around. The five Doms, their submissive flavors of the week, Zach, Gabriel and his small kitchen staff, housekeeping . . . even the landscaping crew that maintained the garden, the lawn, and the pool.

Aiden's cabin, on the other hand, gave a whole new meaning to the word *secluded*. It was halfway up a mountain, with nothing but trees and wild animals around for miles in every direction.

"Well," she said, nudging him with her shoulder. "I hope you're not longing too much for alone time right now."

Aiden chuckled. "Fishing for compliments, Olivia? That's very bratty behavior, you know. And the only way to deal with brats is to spank them."

Laughing, she skipped away from him, closer to the edge of the bluff. "Oh no, whatever shall I do?" she teased in a breathless, damsel-in-distress voice. "Don't spank me, big scary man!"

"Come away from the edge please." He tried to keep his tone light, not wanting to ruin the moment, but there was definitely a hard under-tone in his voice.

She waved a dismissive hand at him. "I'm nowhere close to the edge."

There was a weird twinge in his chest, growing stronger by the second. He had no idea what it was or why it was there. All he knew was he didn't care for it at all. "Olivia—"

"Hold on, I want to get a panoramic picture." Pulling his phone out, she fiddled with the camera settings, then took two steps even closer to the cliff and held it up, sweeping it from left to right, inch by tortuous inch.

Christ, she was close to the edge. A few more steps and she'd go right over. What if she lost her balance, all of her attention on the phone like that? Would he have time to get to her if she toppled over? "I'm not asking you. I'm telling you. Come here right now."

"Almost done . . ."

"Olivia!" He gave up trying to hide the panic raging through him. "Now!"

Her head snapped around, her startled gaze meeting his furious one. She let her arm fall to her side, assuredly ruining her picture. But Aiden didn't fucking care. All that mattered was she remembered who was in charge and did as she was told without further delay.

"I'm sorry," she said, walking toward him. "I didn't realize you were afraid of heights."

"That doesn't fucking matter!" he shouted, gripping her arm hard enough to make her wince. "You don't have to understand my orders, or even agree with them. You only have to follow them. That's what submissives *do*, or did all this fucking around in the woods make you forget that?"

Tears sprang to her sapphire eyes. "I—I'm sorry, Sir. I didn't mean—"

Her words cut off with a small yelp as Aiden dragged her farther away from the cliff edge. "Come," he said, supporting her weight until she got her feet back under her, and she could scurry along beside him. They walked away from the edge about twenty yards, until they got to a fallen tree Olivia had taken several pictures of.

Aiden shoved her in front of him, until her thighs pressed against the large trunk. He dragged her skintight pants down with such force, a seam popped. But he didn't care. He didn't give a fuck if he ripped the things clean off her, and she had to walk back to the Manor naked. It seemed like a fair punishment for what she'd done, in fact.

"Down," he ordered, forcing her to bend over the fallen tree. "Hands behind your head."

She dangled over the trunk without a word of argument or complaint, her hair trailing all the way to the ground. Lacing her fingers behind her head, she waited, shoulders shaking slightly with silent tears.

"Never." Aiden unbuckled his belt. "Disobey me." He pulled it free of his belt loops with a *swoosh* that made Olivia shudder. "Again." Bending the soft, supple leather double and gripping the ends in his right hand, he pushed against her lower back with his left, holding her in place.

He didn't give her any sort of warmup before he started painting her ass red with the belt. "Do you have any idea how fucking scared I was?" he shouted, strapping her again and again and again. The redder her skin got, the better it made him feel. "You could've fallen! You would've *died*! Do *not* make me feel like that again, do you understand me?"

When she didn't respond, he yanked the pants off her completely, taking her sneakers with them, and brought the belt down even harder on the tender flesh at the tops of her thighs. At long last, she sobbed aloud, the sound only egging him on. "I said do you fucking understand me!"

"Yes, Sir, I fucking understand you!" she shouted back, the final word cracking on a sob that shook her entire body.

All the anger drained out of him in that moment, replaced by a cold, numb sensation that started in his chest and spread out to his limbs.

What in the ever-loving fuck was he doing?

The belt fell from Aiden's hand. He didn't even realize he'd dropped it until he heard it hit the ground.

"I'm sorry," he said, hauling her up and spinning her around. Tears streaked down her face, but she was still trying so hard to cry quietly for him. His sweet girl.

"I-I'm s-sorry, too," she said, a hiccup breaking up the words. "I sh-shouldn't have—"

"Oh, Liv." He pulled her against his chest, a gentle hand in her hair, holding her against him. "Shh, don't apologize. I lost my temper. I don't even know what happened—only that I've never been so scared in my life. I don't know what the fuck I was thinking, punishing you when I felt like that." He'd never done anything like it before. Of all the Dominants at the Manor, he was by far the most even-keeled. He'd never even given Stacey Blackwood a *real* punishment, and he'd practically wanted to strangle her.

"Come here," he said, lifting her by her hips until she wrapped her legs around his waist. Then he sat on the fallen tree, in the exact spot where he'd hurt her so unforgivably, cradling her in his lap and rubbing soft circles on her red, swollen skin.

She was clinging to him, looking to him for comfort he didn't deserve to give her anymore. How could she possibly still trust him after that?

"Don't try to hold it in anymore." He whispered it into her ear. "You're allowed to cry."

The sob that came out of her then broke his fucking heart.

CHAPTER 8
Olivia

It was a long time before either of them spoke again. Aiden let her cry herself out, soothing her throbbing flesh with his tender ministrations all the while.

When at last she grew quiet and still, he pushed her gently away, looking down into her eyes. "I'm sorry," he said again, guilt etched into every worried line on his face. He reached up, wiping away her tears with the pads of his thumbs. "Are you all right?"

Grabbing his hand, Olivia slowly lowered it between them, bringing it to the apex of her thighs. He drew in a long, slow breath as his finger slipped easily into her. "Christ," he whispered. He added a second finger, moving them slowly in and out of her. "You're soaked for me."

"Always." She stretched up to plant a kiss on his lips. "Sir."

As he continued to tease her with his fingers, Olivia undid his pants, pushing the offending fabric out of her way until his cock sprang free.

"I don't have a condom with me. I didn't think—"

She silenced him with another kiss, taking him in her hand as she did so. "I don't care. I have an IUD. We saw each other's test results. Fuck me, Aiden." She whispered the words against his lips. "*Please.* I need you."

Grasping her hips again, he lifted her, lowering her carefully onto his cock. She moaned as he filled her inch by painstaking inch. "Christ, you feel so good," he said, digging his fingers into her skin, lifting her up slowly before slamming her back down.

"Aiden," she moaned, licking the salty sheen of sweat from his neck as they fell into a rhythm. "Aiden, Aiden, Aiden . . ."

He captured her lips with his, taking his time with his tongue, just as he was with his cock. It was like he wanted to memorize every inch of her, inside and out.

"Touch yourself for me," he said, nipping at her lower lip. "Show me how you make yourself feel good."

Sucking a finger into her mouth, she made sure it was coated with moisture before she lowered it to her clit, making slow, firm circles.

"Good girl," he rumbled, claiming her mouth with another deep kiss. He tasted faintly of coffee and spearmint, so clean and fresh and perfect that she was practically devouring him. His hands moved from her hips to her ass, sending a new wave of delicious pain through her as he dug his fingers in.

When he eventually picked up the pace, so did she, rubbing frantically at the tiny bud, gasping into his mouth as he kissed her. Oh, God, she was close. So fucking close.

"Fly for me, Liv."

She came completely apart in his arms.

"I need to know something."

Olivia was lying facedown in bed, half asleep as Aiden applied a cool, soothing cream to her bottom and thighs. "What?" she asked sleepily, relishing in the feel of his skin against hers, and the way the cream dulled the worst of the pain from her punishment.

"Why didn't you use your safe word?"

Olivia's eyes popped open. Well, she supposed they had to talk about it eventually. They'd spent the last several hours in a near-constant state of slow, sensual worship. Learning everything about each other's bodies, and all the ways to wring pleasure from each other. In the woods, the garden, the lobby, the enormous bathtub, their bed. Aiden was even delivering this current aftercare with a devotion bordering on reverence.

As much as she would've liked that never to end, it had been a naïve hope.

Sighing, Olivia sat up, holding back a wince as she put weight on her still-swollen bottom. She'd have to take some ibuprofen before bed. "Because I didn't want to."

"You didn't want to?" Aiden asked, disbelief in every word. "Or you didn't remember that you could?"

She tried to lighten the mood with a soft chuckle. "I won't pretend the thought didn't cross my mind," she teased, but it fell flat. His expression remained worried and stony, and she gave up the act. "Yes, I remembered. No, I didn't want to."

Aiden ran a hand through his hair. "Why the fuck not?"

Thinking back to the sheer panic on his face and in his voice out on the cliff, she gave a little shrug and said, "Because I deserved to be punished."

"Not like that! Not when I was furious and out of—"

"Because I trust you," she interrupted.

He snorted, looking away from her. "Well, you fucking shouldn't."

Reaching up, she put her hand against the rough stubble on his cheek, gently pulling until he looked at her again. "But I do."

Aiden rested his hand over hers, closing his eyes as he leaned into her touch. "Why?" So much anguish filled that one word. It made her chest ache.

"Because you're my Dom. Because you're the first person in my entire life who gives a damn about fulfilling *my* wants, *my* needs. You're the first person who ever even bothered to figure out what they were. Do you have any idea how horrible I felt when I realized how much I scared you?"

"That doesn't matter." She started to object, but he didn't give her the chance. "I need you to promise me something. If any Dom ever treats you like I did today, promise me you'll use your safe word and get the fuck out of there. A Dom *always* needs to be calm. He *always* needs to be in control of his emotions, or you could get seriously hurt. Do you hear me?"

"Aiden—"

"*Promise me.*"

Olivia let out a long, slow breath as she gathered her thoughts. "First I want to know why."

His brows furrowed together. "Why I want you to be safe?"

"No, that I understand." She had a strong urge to look away, but made herself hold his gaze as she said, "I want to know why you got so angry. Is it just that you're afraid of heights, or was something else going on?"

Aiden was the one to look away then, though he didn't appear to be upset with her prying. If anything, he looked confused. "I'm not even afraid of heights," he said, his voice soft and low. "Not really."

And it wasn't only that she hadn't listened. If he reacted that way every time a sub disobeyed him, he wouldn't feel so guilty now. Not wanting to distract him as he worked it out in his head, she kept as quiet and still as she could.

When at last he looked at her again, uncertainty still lingered in his eyes. "I don't understand why," he admitted. "All I know is I imagined you falling over the cliff, and I knew I couldn't lose you, too."

"Too?"

Pressing his lips together, he studied her for a long moment, his gaze shuttered. It was obvious he thought he'd said too much. But then he closed his eyes and sighed. "My parents disowned me when they found out I'm in the lifestyle."

Olivia's chest ached at the pain in his voice. Reaching out, she laid a gentle hand on his arm. "How did they find out?"

"I told them," he said, scoffing. "I know, stupid, right? It's not like it was a surprise when they freaked the fuck out. That's why I kept it a secret for so long." He ran his hand through his hair again, making it stand up that time. "To give you an idea of the type of people they are, they'd been trying to get me to marry some appropriately virginal girl from their church for over a year when I finally snapped and told them *why* I kept saying no. Ten minutes later, I wasn't their son anymore."

"Jesus. That's so fucked up." She gave his arm a comforting squeeze.

Shitty parents were at least something she could understand and commiserate with. "When was this?"

"Seven years ago. Jonathan, Leo, and Mason had just sold their startup for about a bajillion dollars, and we were all getting serious about opening the Manor. We'd been talking about it for years, but suddenly it felt possible."

Olivia didn't know who Leo was, but the rest was old news. Plenty of girls in r/SordidFairfordAffairs had Googled the various Doms, and Olivia had read all about the startup two of the partners had sold, though she couldn't remember exactly what the company did. Something to do with bioengineering, maybe.

With a halfhearted shrug, Aiden said, "So I guess I was about to have to tell them anyway. I couldn't exactly hide being partial owner of a luxury resort—not with them all up in my business every second of the day." His grimace etched lines into his forehead too deep for a man in his mid-thirties. "And I know them. They would've insisted on visiting whenever they wanted, and then what? We'd cancel all the reservations and hide everything in the basement? It would've been fucking absurd."

"They put you in an impossible position," she said, leaning her head against his arm, hoping her touch would soothe him. "There was literally no way for you to win, so you took control of the situation. Made everything happen on your terms. It sounds like the best possible choice to me."

He let out a long, slow breath. "I . . . I've never thought of it like that." She could practically hear the gears turning in his head as he considered. "You might be right. I was definitely sick and fucking tired of pretending by then, that's for sure. You have no idea how hard I tried to fit their ideal of the perfect son when I was little. But it was never enough. *Never.*"

A solitary tear made its way down Olivia's right cheek. His pain resonated in the most damaged parts of her heart.

"So if I was going to fail anyway, I might as well embrace being a— what was it again? Oh, yeah." Making air quotes, he spat out, "A perverted monster that'll rot in hell for all eternity."

Olivia winced. Why did parents have to be so cruel? "Aiden, I'm so sorry. You didn't deserve any of that."

"It's okay," he said, tone almost flippant now. "It was a long time ago."

Olivia understood the sudden change. It was easier to pretend it didn't really matter than to cut yourself wide open so others could watch you bleed. She would know—it was how she usually spoke about her own family.

"And don't think I didn't notice you changing the subject," Aiden said, nudging her until she sat up again. "I'm the one trying to comfort and help you, remember? You're the one who got hurt *today*."

She'd really been hoping to distract him for longer. Maybe even forever. Alas. "Did you forget everything that happened after my punishment?"

"I . . ." He blinked a couple of times, clearly not expecting her answer.

"When I saw how panicked you were, the guilt was overwhelming. I felt so selfish. So cruel."

He let out a frustrated groan. "But you're neither of those things."

"Maybe not. But it's how I felt. I've hated myself so many times in my life, and do you know what happened every other time?"

With a little sigh, he shook his head.

"I kept right on hating myself. I fell into a depression spiral I didn't know how to get out of." She waited until he was looking her in the eye. "I've seen five different therapists. Tried nearly every anxiety and depression medication there is. I've spent the last decade trying to figure out how to do what you did in under ten minutes. So please don't try to tell me that was anything but exactly what I needed, whether you realized it at the time or not."

Some of the tension went out of his shoulders, and she knew he finally understood. "You're remarkable. Do you know that?"

Her smile was a feeble, delicate thing. "All I am is a broken girl, putting myself back together one piece at a time. And I'm not particularly good at it, either."

Aiden pulled her in close, holding her until she started to feel safe again. "Let me help."

CHAPTER 9
Aiden

Frowning down at his laptop, Aiden concentrated on the very important letter he was typing.

Dear Olivia,

I want to fuck you senseless. After that, I'll spank you until you fall apart in my arms, and then fuck you again until you fall apart even more.

You have the most spectacular ass I've ever seen in my life. It's the perfect heart shape, absolutely MADE for spanking. And the way you clench your cheeks together when you're waiting for the next stroke, but then force yourself to relax because you know it's what I want of you . . . I'm getting hard just thinking about it.

You're perfect.

Blah blah blah blah blah, I need to keep looking like I'm busy for a little bit longer. Jesus fucking Christ, you look sexy in that dress. I can't wait to take it off of you.

Yours, endlessly,

Aiden

Of course, he didn't really need to write Olivia a letter. She was standing all of ten feet away from him, fidgeting in her way-too-short French maid's uniform as she flitted about the study with a feather duster. But their current little game required him to concentrate on his computer, so he figured he might as well do something entertaining rather than hit a bunch of random keys.

Aiden read over the ridiculous missive, his gaze stopping on, "You're perfect." He hadn't entirely meant to type that. Well, he hadn't technically *meant* to type any of it. He'd simply let his fingers spell out whatever random thoughts popped into his head.

He frowned at his laptop screen again, and this time it wasn't part of his act. He'd been active on the scene since college, when Jonathan and Leo had shown him a spanking video online and changed his entire life. And he'd been taking guests at the Manor for the last five years, putting the number of women he'd dominated through all that time well into the dozens. And he'd certainly never found himself thinking, intentionally or otherwise, that any of those other women were perfect.

What the fuck was he supposed to do with a thought like that, exactly? It's not like they were going to ride off into the sunset together, spanking and fucking their way to happily ever after. She had a whole life down near Boston, with a job and an apartment and friends. A life she certainly wouldn't give up to live in the Vermont wilderness with him—and what? Sit around waiting while he dominated other women for money?

And he wasn't pulling a Leo and giving up Fairford Manor anytime soon. No fucking way. He'd been in a bit of a slump lately, sure, but he was still living his dream life.

Besides, Leo's family was old money, as was his wife Sophie's. What was Aiden supposed to do, give up his new luxurious lifestyle, sell his cabin, and go back to flipping houses?

No, he needed to remember this was nothing but his job. Olivia was there to get a service from him, which he was happy to provide for a sizeable fee. There was nothing more to think about. Period.

Closing the file without saving it, Aiden shut his laptop and looked up at his squirming submissive. She was still trying to pull the ruffled skirt of her dress down to cover her ass, which was an exercise in futility if ever there was one. She'd barely even touched the shelves of books he'd ordered her to dust. "Olivia, come here," he said, letting a note of sternness slip into his voice.

She jumped, almost toppling sideways in her three-inch fuck-me heels. It was a struggle to keep himself from chuckling, but he managed it. The poor thing obviously wasn't used to wearing shoes like those, and he didn't want to embarrass her.

Worry wrinkled Olivia's brow as she walked around the desk to where he sat. "Is everything all right, Mr. McLaren?" she asked.

Aiden regarded her with what he considered his Disappointed Dom Face, and was delighted when a shiver passed through her. "What did I tell you about your uniform?"

Her shoulders slumped. "That it's exactly the length you want it to be, Sir."

"Well, then," he said, standing and removing his suit jacket, "I'm interested to hear why you keep trying to pull it down despite my very clear wishes."

"I—I wasn't—"

"I wouldn't finish that sentence if I were you," he interrupted, giving her a hard look until she lowered her gaze to her feet. "I don't think you want to find out what happens to naughty maids who lie to their employers." Removing his cufflinks, he dropped them onto the desk and began rolling up his sleeves.

Watching his hands as they worked, she flushed a deep, beautiful red. "I'm sorry, Sir." Her voice was high and breathy. What was it about a Dom rolling up his sleeves that got every submissive in the world so hot and bothered? Aiden wasn't sure he'd ever understand.

"Not as sorry as you're about to be." He held out an expectant hand. "Give me your panties. You've lost the privilege of wearing them."

Her gaze flew up to meet his. "Oh, no Sir! I'm so sorry! I won't do it again! Please, let me—"

"*Your panties*, Olivia. You're in enough trouble as it is. Don't try my patience."

"Oh, Mr. McLaren, please." The quiver in her voice made his cock harden. "What will the other maids think?"

Aiden absolutely loved roleplay, so long as his partner was able to get into it properly. He'd been with his fair share of subs who giggled at every little thing, or else were so ridiculously over-the-top it pulled him right out of the scene. But when he'd read in Olivia's application that she liked to plug her own ass before cleaning her apartment, pretending she was being punished by her Dom, he had a feeling she'd be a natural at this little game.

He was anything but disappointed.

"They'll think"—he grasped her arm, pulling her down over his lap as he sat, earning a surprised squeak—"you're a naughty little girl who needed to be punished. Which is exactly what you are, so why shouldn't they think it?" He flipped her skirt up, revealing ruffled white panties beneath, not the usual black lace she favored. He'd chosen them as part of her costume that morning, loving the idea of something so sweet and innocent on his sexy little anal slut.

Olivia's whole body trembled as he pulled her panties down to her mid-thighs, brushing the back of his hand against her skin as he did so. "I'm sorry, Sir," she said again, her voice little more than a whisper.

"It's too late for that," he admonished, shifting her body into exactly the position he wanted. "Now I expect you to accept your punishment with grace if you wish to remain in my employ. Do you understand?"

She sniffed. "Yes, Sir."

"Your hands and feet will touch the ground at all times. I'm only going to give you thirty, as you're new and perhaps didn't understand how I run my household. But if your hands or feet ever leave the ground, we're starting over. And we'll keep doing so until you obey. Understood?"

"Y-yes, Sir," she said, moving into the demanded position, and it sounded like she was holding back tears.

Beautiful. Absolutely beautiful. He hadn't roleplayed with anyone so good in years, if ever. He rewarded her by bringing his hand down hard across both her cheeks, one right after the other.

Olivia gave a small shout of surprise, her whole body jerking in response to the unexpected pain.

"That's not a very good start, is it?" Aiden scolded as she hurried to return her toes and fingertips to the carpet.

"I'm so sorry, Mr. McLaren," she said, sounding as deeply remorseful as if he'd caught her stealing from him. How much of it was acting, and how much was her natural, desperate need to please him? "I didn't realize we were starting. It won't happen again."

Resting a hand across her ass, he gave a disappointed sigh. "See that it doesn't. While I'm perfectly willing to spank you all day and night if that's what it takes to bring you in line, this house needs cleaning, and I'm an extremely busy man."

Her ass clenched underneath his hand, then relaxed again, exactly as he'd written in his letter. With her facedown over his lap, little more than the antique Persian rug in view, he allowed himself a small smile.

"Now," he said, lifting his hand. "Let's start again, shall we?"

When he brought his hand down that time, she stayed in perfect position. "Good girl," he said, and all her muscles relaxed at his words. "Twenty-nine more to go."

He peppered her ass with several quick spanks in a row, building up in intensity with each one. Pausing after stroke number fifteen, he rubbed a few slow, gentle circles against her reddening skin. "Halfway there, Olivia," he told her, and she only whimpered in response. "The final fifteen will be much harder. Prepare yourself."

Her fingers clenched into the thick rug before straightening out again. "I'll be good, Sir. I promise."

With no additional warning, he raised his hand and started in on the second half of her spanking. He took his time, watching her ass as it reverberated under his hand, then turned a darker shade of red with each crushing impact. Though Olivia's low wail started at stroke twenty-four and didn't stop until he was again rubbing her punished cheeks, she didn't move her hands or feet again.

It was fun to prolong a punishment when his sub wasn't able to follow his instructions (so long as she wasn't doing it on purpose . . . brats were a whole different story). But nothing pleased him more than when a sub did exactly as she was told. Especially when it was genuinely hard for her.

Grasping her around the waist, Aiden lifted Olivia up, settling her on his lap. He had planned to praise her for her obedience, but when he looked into her flushed, lust-filled face, he instead found himself asking, "No tears?" He made a tsking noise. "I clearly haven't punished you enough."

A startled look stole over her lovely features, but she hid it quickly enough. "I'm sorry to disappoint you again, Sir." She bit her bottom lip, no longer meeting his gaze. "Please punish me more. I deserve it."

With a decisive nod, Aiden stood, lifting her up with him. "Come," he said, leading her around the desk with a hand gripped tightly in her hair. She stumbled at first, the panties still around her thighs impeding her steps. But then the ruffled white silk fell to the ground, and she stepped out of them, obediently hurrying along next to him. When they reached the other side, Aiden bent her down over the desk.

Olivia sighed softly as her stomach and breasts pressed against the smooth wood. As if being bent over furniture brought her a sense of calm and peace.

Given how submissive she was, Aiden suspected it probably did.

Loosening his tie, he used it to bind her wrists behind her back, trapping her skirt beneath her arms to keep it out of the way. "Spread your legs wider," he ordered.

She shuffled her feet to either side, hardly moving them more than an inch.

"*Wider*," he said again, using his own leg between her thighs to gently guide her into the exact position he wanted. When he was done, he stepped back, surveying his work.

Her bare ass was on spectacular display, her spread legs giving him full view of her pussy and her asshole. The stiletto heels added enough length to her legs that her waist was slightly above the desk, which left her ass elevated, practically begging for more punishment.

With great difficulty, Aiden pulled his gaze away from her perfect ass and up to her face. Her left cheek rested on the desktop, her eyes closed tight, and her breath came in short, hard bursts.

"What's your safe word, Olivia?" Aiden asked, moving in beside her and putting a gentle hand on her hip.

"Orchid, Sir."

"Do you wish you use it now?"

Her eyes clenched even tighter. "No, Sir. Not at all."

He frowned down at her as he considered her answer. Her breathing sounded very much like when she'd started to panic down in the dungeon on their first night. Only she'd been pale and wild-eyed then, not flushed and still and obedient.

Needing the sanity check, Aiden slipped two fingers into her cunt. "Mmm," he said, slowly moving them in and out. "You seem to be enjoying your punishment a little too much."

When Olivia moaned, his worries slipped away. She wasn't hyperventilating. She was so turned on she'd started panting.

Ignoring the profound ache in his cock that ordered him to drive into her hot, tight pussy and never stop, he backed away. "Don't move," he instructed. "You will stay here, bound and spread and waiting for me, while I go get what I need to finish your punishment." He could probably find what he wanted in the desk drawers, but this would be so much more fun.

Her hands clenched into tight fists, and her breathing came even faster, but all she said was, "Yes, Sir."

"If anyone finds you while I'm gone, tell them you're waiting for your Dom to return. They'll know not to touch you without my consent. Do you understand?"

"I understand, Sir." The words were little more than a gasp.

Unable to help himself, Aiden grinned as he left the room. He hadn't failed to notice her reaction when he'd said the other Manor Doms would need *his* consent to touch her, not *hers*. The muscles in her ass and thighs had instantly tightened, as if she longed to squeeze her legs together.

Her application made it clear she had fantasies about being shared with multiple men. But fantasy and reality didn't always line up, and he was exceptionally glad their kinks were once again in perfect sync.

Hurrying upstairs, Aiden let himself into their room, rummaging around in the dresser for what he wanted. The drawers were full of plugs and paddles, cuffs and chains, and everything else he could want.

After making his selections, he took his time going downstairs, knowing the longer wait would drive her mad in the best possible way. With any luck, one of the others *would* discover her on display in the study. If so, her arousal would be dripping down her thighs by the time he made it back to her.

He was deep into a reverie of what he was about to do to her when he turned the corner to the back hallway. A voice drifted out of the study—a voice that didn't belong to Olivia or one of the other Doms.

It was the high, nasally voice of Stacey Blackwood.

"Shit," he said under his breath, hurrying his steps. When at last he could decipher what his former guest was saying, he was only a few feet away from the doorway.

"—anyone would ever want to look at your fat ass is beyond me. Let alone fuck you. I bet Aiden took one look at your picture and decided to charge you double."

Aiden was about to storm into the room and give Stacey a piece of his mind, but Olivia spoke before he got the chance: "I'm waiting for my Dom to return." She said it in a bland, robotic voice, and pride swelled in his chest.

His strong, spectacularly submissive girl. He should've known Olivia wouldn't let the bitter words of that jealous bitch touch her. Given what she'd written in her application, Aiden wasn't sure what to do next. Swoop in and come to her rescue? Or let her prove to herself how much of an amazing badass she truly was?

"I bet you'll be waiting a long time. You know why he left you here like this, don't you?" Somehow, her voice got even crueler. "He wanted to humiliate you while he went to find someone worth fucking. He hopes you'll be so embarrassed you'll leave early."

"I'm waiting for my Dom to return."

"I think I'll go find him. Once he sees me, it could be hours before he remembers where he left you." She gave a nasty laugh. "I sure hope you're comfortable."

Olivia took in a long, shuddering breath, letting it out before she answered. "I'm waiting for my Dom to return." There was a slight quiver in her voice that time. He'd let things go too far.

Without another moment's hesitation, he stepped into the room. "Stacey, that's quite enough."

The tall, thin blonde whipped around, eyes wide. Her shock morphed into what he supposed was meant to be a shy, seductive smile as soon as she saw him. "Oh, *Aiden*, it's you," she purred, walking up and running a single finger down his chest. "I was just coming to look for you."

"I can't imagine why," he said, taking hold of her wrist and jerking her hand away. "Or have you forgotten Jonathan is your Dominant this week?"

"Oh, he won't mind," she said, trying to press up against him. "Trust me. He knows all about our history together."

Releasing her wrist, Aiden stepped away before she could reach him. "Stacey, stop. Now."

She pouted—something she'd spent about half of their week together doing. It made him grind his teeth together. "But why?" she whined, then seemed to think better of it. She looked up at him through her eyelashes, trying again for a seductive smile. "What we had was incredible. Don't you want to experience it again?"

Aiden closed his eyes and let out a long sigh. He should've black-listed her rather than pawning her off on someone else. The money they could get from Stacey or her socialite friends wasn't worth all this hassle.

"I have tried to be polite," he said, only reopening his eyes after the words were out. He met her gaze with the stoniest expression he could, wanting her to finally get the hint. "But you force me to be rude. No, I don't want to experience it again. If I did, I would be your host this week instead of Jonathan. I'm sorry I didn't feel the same connection you did, but I hope Jonathan helps you enjoy the rest of your stay. Now I'm going to have to ask you to leave, as you said some terrible things to my sub, who's waiting for me."

They stared at each other for several long, tense seconds. Aiden was starting to think he'd have to physically force her out the door, but then she turned on her heel, her long hair hitting him in the chest, and stalked silently from the room, back ramrod straight.

As soon as Stacey crossed the threshold, Aiden shut and locked the study door. By the time he got to Olivia, she had her face pressed against the desk, and her whole body was shaking.

"I'm here," he said, untying the knot at her wrists as quickly as he could. Helping her up with gentle hands on her arms, he turned her to face him. Silent tears streamed down her face, and she wouldn't meet his gaze. "Oh, Liv, I'm so sorry." She collapsed against him then, and he scooped her into his arms, carrying her over to an armchair.

Holding her against his chest and stroking her hair, he let her cry herself out. "It's all right," he said when at last her tears were drying up. "Nothing she said was true. You're beautiful, and smart, and funny, and kind, and a hundred times more submissive than she could ever dream of being. I've been happier these last few days than I can remember being in years, all because of *you*."

Finally, she looked into his eyes. There was so much pain there. But also hope.

"And between you and me," he said conspiratorially, looking around as if he might be overheard, "my week with that jealous, stuck-up brat was literal torture."

When she smiled, it was like sunlight emerging at the end of a thunderstorm. In that moment, he would've promised her the world if it would keep her smiling.

"I know I shouldn't listen to anything she says," Olivia said, her voice hoarse after so much crying. "And I don't usually let mean girl bullshit affect me. It's just . . ." She seemed unable to go on, as if her throat had closed up.

"You alluded to some things in your application." Aiden spoke slowly, picking his words with care. "About your childhood. Is that what this is about?"

She tried to speak, failed, and shrugged instead, gaze firmly planted on his chest.

"You don't have to talk about it if you're not ready," Aiden said, giving her forehead a soft kiss. "In fact, you don't have to talk about it at all if that's what you want. Though I do think it might help." It had felt like a hundred-pound weight lifting off his chest when he'd confided in Olivia the night before.

It took her a few tries, but she finally managed to get out, "Later. Maybe. If I can . . ." She sighed. "Maybe."

"Zero pressure," he assured her, gently guiding her head down to rest against his chest again. "This week is all about you, and what you need, remember? Promise me you won't forget it."

She relaxed against him so completely, it made his heart skip a beat. "I won't."

CHAPTER 10
Olivia

A iden was reticent to let Olivia leave their room again after the whole fiasco in the study. As Chef Gabriel was happy to have his delectable meals delivered to their room, they didn't *need* to venture out. Particularly since the dresser was literally filled with sex toys, bondage gear, and spanking paraphernalia. If Aiden had made it his personal mission to ensure Olivia got experience with every single one of them, with baths and full-body massages and other heavenly aftercare in between . . . well, she wasn't going to complain.

At least not at first. After over twenty-four hours secluded in their suite, however, Olivia had a serious case of cabin fever.

So what if that asshole was out there somewhere, roaming the halls? Was she going to let that rob her of getting the absolute most out of her stay? There were *dozens* of things she still wanted to try in the dungeon, though Aiden would never agree to that as their first little field trip. Better to start with something small and innocent, like the pool.

Olivia had spent the last hour convincing Aiden to go. It had involved a lot of begging, mostly on her knees, and not always with words. At last, he had relented, and she was almost giddy as they stepped through the ornate French doors at the back of the house.

They crossed the flagstone patio to a lovely, sprawling flower garden with perfectly pruned square hedges. Olivia couldn't help glancing at a wrought iron bench in a little alcove to their left as they passed. A blush heated her cheeks as she remembered Aiden bending her over the side and fucking her ass on the way back from their hike, as a gardener worked nearby. Surreptitiously, she ran a finger across the long bruise on her pelvis, from where he'd slammed her into the iron armrest over and over.

Olivia shivered in the most delicious way. How was this her life? Her first four days at the Manor had been more glorious than she ever could've dreamed. If only she'd built up the nerve sooner.

And if only she wasn't terrified of losing her nerve again the moment she left Manor grounds.

Sliding his arm around her shoulders, Aiden leaned down to whisper in her ear. "I see you staring at that bench, little girl. Are you looking for a repeat performance?"

She grinned up at him. "Just remembering. Though I am, of course, yours to command."

"Mmm," Aiden said, moving his hand down to squeeze her sore bottom. "Good answer."

He didn't steer them off the main path, though. Instead, he slipped his hand beneath her skimpy bikini bottoms and led them straight toward the soft sounds of splashing and voices, fondling her the whole way. It didn't help matters that he wore nothing but swim trunks, his chiseled abs on glorious display. Olivia was about ready to drag him off the path and jump on him by the time they reached the pool gate.

And he was definitely smirking, the jerk. He knew exactly what he was doing to her.

"Here we are," Aiden said as he opened the gate for her, sounding completely unaffected. He finally let go of her ass as she passed through, giving it a firm swat on her way by.

The other four people occupying the pool looked up when she yelped in surprise, making her blush all over again. Not exactly the cool, sexy entrance she would've preferred.

"I was wondering if we'd ever meet properly," said one of the men— the tall, lean one she'd seen on her first night. His gaze flicked over to

Aiden. "I haven't seen either of you since the other night in the dungeon. Where have you been keeping her hidden?"

"We've been occupied." Aiden gave the two girls in the pool a flirty wink. "I'm sure you ladies understand." The two women looked at each other, then erupted into delighted giggles.

For one, fleeting moment, Olivia wondered if she should be jealous. Aiden had always been cold—even downright hostile—toward that Stacey woman. She'd sort of expected him to treat all the other female guests the same way. But looking at the gorgeous women in the pool, she found herself imagining Aiden deep in a scene with the pair of them instead.

She resisted the urge to squeeze her thighs together as Aiden wrapped his arm around her again, tugging her up against his side. "This," he said, kissing the top of her head, "is Olivia. She's new to the scene, but might very well be the most naturally submissive person I've ever met. I haven't been able to keep my hands off her for days."

Olivia melted against him, basking in his words like they were sunshine.

"I'm glad to hear she lives up to all your hype," the second Dom in the pool said, then turned his boyish grin on Olivia. "Zach tells me he's been carrying around your application since January, pining over his perfect sub."

Olivia's mouth fell open, though she snapped it immediately shut again. She didn't want Aiden to see. Besides, there was no way that was true.

Was there?

"Oh, shut up," Aiden said, though he didn't sound upset. "Are you two idiots going to introduce yourselves and your subs, or do I have to do all the work around here?"

The Dom she'd seen in the dungeon spoke first. "I'm Mason St. John. I'm one of the founders of Fairford Manor, along with Jonathan and Aiden." He inclined his head to Aiden, who did the same in return. Then he gestured toward the petite redhead at his side. "And this is Tara. She's—"

"Master Mason's very most favorite client," she finished for him, earning a scathing look from her Dom. Not seeming to notice, she giggled again. "This is my fifth time coming to the Manor, and Master Mason has chosen me every time." She beamed up at Olivia, puffing out her already sizeable chest in pride.

"And yet," Mason said softly, wrapping Tara's long, straight hair around his fist, "being here with your friend has clearly made you forget your manners. Perhaps another visit to the dungeon with Master Rafe is in order."

All the color drained from the girl's face, and Olivia couldn't blame her. From what she'd read online, Rafe was only for the hardest of hardcore subs. She had a feeling he'd been the one giving his poor sub twenty-five stripes with a rattan cane.

"I'm sorry, Master," Tara said, all the excitement gone from her voice. "Please punish me yourself. Don't give me to *him*."

Mason didn't answer, nor did he immediately dole out a punishment. Though he did keep his fist in her hair, forcing her to arch her neck. He motioned for the other Dom to continue the introductions.

"Well, this is Tara's friend, Liz. It's her first time here, too. Guess she finally got sick of Tara having all the fun and decided to tag along. Lucky me." He reached over and pinched Liz's left nipple, making her moan. "And I'm Camden."

As she'd suspected from his goofy grin: Camden Reid, the resident fuckboy. From what Olivia had read, the three things he loved most were fucking, spanking, and blow jobs, in that order. Real pain didn't do much for him, and neither did tears. The partners had brought him in for the guests who wanted something lighter than what they wanted to dole out.

"So," Camden said, "are you two getting in, or did you just stop by for a chat?"

His grin was infectious, and Olivia found herself returning it as she and Aiden climbed into the pool. The water was heated to a perfect temperature, and she sighed happily as she slipped into it up to her neck. The cabana-like chaises and assortment of big, leafy plants arranged around the water transformed the place into a spectacular oasis. It would've been a magical place to fool around with Aiden; the other occupants hadn't exactly figured into her plans.

Not wanting to seem rude or standoffish, she turned to Liz and asked, "Are you new to the scene, too, or only new to the Manor?"

"The Manor," she answered, her smile kind and encouraging. "Tara and I know each other from our dungeon in Atlanta. We both started playing there a few years ago, right after we graduated college. I was tired of her having all the bragging rights with the other subs, so I came along this time."

"Master, may I speak to her?" Tara asked in a timid voice.

Giving her an approving look, Mason loosened his grip enough for her to straighten her neck. "You may."

Excitement flashed through Tara's green eyes again as she blurted, "You have to tell us *all* about yourself. How did you hear about the Manor if you're brand new? And have you really never done anything at all? Like, *anything*? God, I don't know how you've survived so long!" She gasped, her bright eyes going round. "Not that I'm calling you old! I mean, you're obviously older than me, but you're not *old* old. Please don't be angry?" She couldn't seem to decide whether to look at Olivia or her Dom.

Mason's expression was one of utter resignation, which only made the whole thing even funnier. Unable to help herself, Olivia laughed. "I'm not angry at all. Please don't worry."

The younger woman's shoulders slumped in relief. "Oh, thank God."

"You'll have to get used to Tara," Liz said, grinning. "She gives the term 'word vomit' a whole new meaning."

"If you think this is bad, you should hear me when I come," Tara said gloomily.

They all laughed at that—even the reserved Mason—and Olivia finally relaxed into the conversation. "To answer your questions," she said, "I heard about the Manor online. Yes, I really am brand new to all of this, but I've thought about it and desperately wanted it since I was seventeen."

"You knew even before I did!" Tara sounded scandalized. "I found out when my college boyfriend spanked me. He was just being silly, but I basically jumped his bones three seconds later." She laughed, the memory clearly bringing her pleasure. "How about you?"

Olivia found herself marveling at how open Tara was. As if there wasn't a thing in the world that could embarrass her. It was infectious. "My best friend in high school found a kinky book in her mom's nightstand. She read part of it out loud to me as a joke, thinking I'd find it hilarious like she did. I pretended I agreed with her, but I snuck back and read more of it on my own later." Her clit was pulsing just thinking about that book. "Nothing had ever made me feel like that before."

Cocking her head to one side, Liz asked, "Why haven't you done anything about it before now?"

"Anxiety." The other girls gave her sympathetic looks, and Olivia shrugged. "It's kept me from trying a lot of new things in my life." Like finding new friends, or moving until she discovered a place she actually loved, or even getting a job that fulfilled her instead of exasperating her.

Or giving relationships another shot.

The risk of making things worse instead of better had kept her exactly where she was.

"But I'm here now, and that's what matters."

"Fuck yeah," Camden agreed. "I hope Aiden is making all your deepest, darkest fantasies come true."

Olivia looked up at her Dom with a shy smile. "No complaints so far."

Aiden smirked at his two colleagues, which made the girls start giggling all over again.

"Tell us one you haven't done yet," Tara urged, her nipples tightening despite the warm water. "A really, really filthy one."

"Tara," Mason said warningly.

But now Camden and Liz were watching her expectantly, excitement in their eyes. Even Aiden was staring down at her, waiting.

"Well," Olivia said, drawing the word out. "I—I guess there is one I have a lot that we, uh . . . that we haven't tried at all. Since we've mostly been alone."

She finally had Mason's full attention, too.

"Oh, *fuck* yes," Camden said, that adorable fuckboy grin back in place.

"*Ooooh,*" Tara crooned at the same time, looking up at Mason with a sweet, pleading little pout. "Master, you have to help her. Please say you will."

Giving his sub an indulgent look, Mason said, "She hasn't even told us what the fantasy is yet."

Tara rolled her eyes sky high. "Oh, please. Whatever it is, it obviously involves multiple dicks." Belatedly, she tacked on, "Master."

"You're itching for a caning, aren't you?" Mason said, staring down his nose at her. Tara ducked her head, but Olivia could see the small smile she was trying to hide.

"She does have a point, though," Liz said, her brown eyes still flashing with excitement. "So Olivia, how many dicks do you need?"

Olivia was quite sure she flushed from the tips of her toes all the way up to the top of her head. This was the most mortifying conversation *of her life*.

Before she could even begin to form a response that wouldn't make her die on the spot, Aiden cleared his throat, drawing all eyes to him. "While I appreciate your . . . *enthusiasm*, ladies, as her Dom, it's my job to determine what Olivia needs and see that she gets it."

Oh, thank God and holy Jesus. Perhaps she'd live to fuck another day after all.

"Gentlemen, if I could speak to you a moment," he continued, motioning for the other Doms to follow him to the far end of the pool.

As soon as they were gone, Tara and Liz converged on her. "*Girrrrl*, you are about to get fucked in the best possible way," Tara whispered, bouncing up and down. "Can we watch? We won't stay if you don't want us to, but *please* say you don't mind!"

"Trust me," Liz said, giving Olivia's hardened nipples a pointed look. "She doesn't mind." She looped her arm through Olivia's, bumping shoulders with her. "Us girls who like an audience have to stick together."

"Good thinking! Any chance you live close to Atlanta?" Tara linked arms with them both, so they formed a conspiratorial little kink triangle. "If you do, you *have* to come to our club! We can all—"

But Olivia didn't get a chance to learn any of Tara's plans, or to let them know she wasn't from anywhere near Georgia. All three men had climbed out of the pool, and now stood at the edge, looking down at their subs with their very sternest Dom faces. "I think that's enough of that," Mason said, drawing their attention.

"Olivia, come," Aiden said, motioning to the ladder at his feet.

"Good luck," Liz whispered as Olivia swam away.

She was only on the second rung when hands grasped both her arms, and Aiden and Camden lifted her the rest of the way out of the water. She tried not to panic as they led her to an enormous, cushioned chaise, though her heart felt like it would beat right out of her chest.

Meanwhile, Mason had turned to the two subs still in the pool. "We've decided you can stay and watch, but on two conditions. First, that one of you loan us your bikini top so we can use it to restrain Ms. Adams."

Olivia craned her neck in time to see both women remove their tops as quickly as they could, throwing them onto the pool deck. The sodden garments landed near Mason's feet with a loud *plop*, splashing water on him.

"Thank you," Mason said, a touch sarcastically, as he shook the water off his legs. "And second, you must make each other come at least as many times as Olivia."

"Thank you, Master," Tara said, snaking her arm around her friend's waist. "Oh, thank you, thank you, *thank you*." Liz looked equally pleased with the deal.

With a satisfied nod, Mason picked up Tara's bright green bikini top, wrung it out over the pool, and strolled leisurely toward the chaise where Olivia was now reclined, a Dom on either side of her.

Olivia's heart was pounding so hard, she was sure she was about to have a panic attack. Could she actually do this? Or was this one of those fantasies best left in the realm of self-pleasure, never to see the light of day?

When Mason took firm hold of her wrists and began binding them together in front of her, she jerked her hands away, unable to help herself.

"Olivia," Aiden said, without a hint of the anger she'd expected. "Look at me."

Grateful for an easy order to follow, she did as she was told, losing herself in the utter calm radiating from his deep brown eyes.

"I'll never ask you to do something I think you can't handle. You know that, right?"

Her heart rate was already slowing down. "Yes, Sir."

"Do you trust me to take care of you?"

She took a deep breath, then let it out just as slowly. He was right. She could do this. "Yes, Sir. Always."

When one corner of his mouth quirked up, he seemed almost surprised by his own reaction. His expression returned to his patient Dom face a moment later. "Then be a good girl and hold out your hands for Mason."

With one more calming breath, Olivia did as she was told. Mason bound her hands tightly, tying the wet spandex into an intense-looking knot. Then three sets of hands were picking at the strings of her own bikini, undoing the little bows she'd obsessed over tying exactly right, wanting to be perfect for her Dom. All her hard work was undone in seconds, and the skimpy bits of fabric were tossed aside without a thought.

Olivia was comfortable with her body most of the time, but she'd also never been naked in front of three men at once. And with an audience to boot—something she could hardly forget with a neon green bikini top wrapped around her wrists. It took all her self-control to keep herself from trying to cover up with her arms and hands, though her pussy clearly didn't get the message from her brain. She could feel the wetness between her thighs.

"Mmm," Aiden said, reaching down to plump up her breasts, her bound arms squeezing them in a tawdry display. "She has such beautiful breasts. Don't you agree?"

"Lovely." Mason reached down to give one nipple a harsh tweak, making her gasp. "Though I know what would make them even lovelier."

Aiden pinched the other nipple even harder, and it set off a corresponding ache in her pussy. She squeezed her legs together, hoping a little pressure would help, but it only made her feel emptier. "An excellent notion," Aiden said, watching her squirm with heavy-lidded eyes. "Camden, if you would."

Grinning, Camden went to a large wicker chest she'd assumed held towels. But when he pried the lid open, it was full of sex toys (because of course it was). He only rummaged around for a few seconds before he returned, a tiny, sealed bottle of lube in one hand, alligator-style nipple clamps in the other.

"Be a good girl and present your breasts to us," Aiden said, lust deepening his voice.

Olivia arched her back, propping up her breasts even more with her arms. Then Mason took hold of one nipple and Aiden the other, both men squeezing and pulling mercilessly before attaching the clamps Camden handed them. Screwing her eyes closed, she sucked in a harsh breath at the burst of sharp pain.

"What a good girl you've brought for us to play with," Mason said, giving one of the clamps a little tug and making her whimper. His hands moved lower, taking hold of her hips, and her eyes flew open as he flipped her over. He arranged her exactly as he wanted her, like she was nothing but a large doll—on her knees with her ass in the air, bent all the way down until her forehead pressed into the chaise cushion.

When cold lube dribbled into the crack of her ass, she let out an embarrassingly loud moan.

Camden chuckled. "You weren't kidding. She really is a little anal slut."

The words were like a direct line to her clit, but Mason had positioned her with her legs spread, and there was nothing she could do about it. The throbbing in her clit and pussy got even worse when one of them gathered the lube onto two fingers and started pumping them in and out of her rear hole. "*Please*," she begged, not caring which of them answered her plea. She was sure if they touched her clit for even a second, she would come.

All three of them chuckled that time, and it didn't sound like they had any intention of showing her mercy. "Wait until it's Aiden's cock and not my fingers," Camden said, giving his fingers a ruthless twist that left her gasping. "We're just getting started, baby."

When he removed his thick fingers entirely, Olivia almost cried out at the loss. Though she didn't suffer for long. Strong hands were on her shoulders and hips again, lifting her to stand at the end of the chaise.

Now completely nude, Camden plopped down into the spot she'd vacated and laced his fingers behind his head, grinning up at Olivia.

Not that she was looking at his face. Sweet merciful Jesus, his cock was fucking enormous. She watched with greedy eyes as he rolled a condom down over it. Afraid she might have legit drooled, she licked the corners of her lips and hoped no one noticed.

She was so distracted by Camden's erection, she jumped when Aiden and Mason took hold of her again. They helped her kneel over Camden, straddling his hips, her bound hands splayed on his hard chest. Jesus Christ, she was fucking panting again, and there wasn't even anyone inside her yet.

"So eager," Camden said, giving both nipple clamps a none-too-gentle pull. "Good, eager little girls get fucked *hard*. Is that what you want, baby?"

"*Yes.*" She practically breathed the word. A sharp spank on her left ass cheek had her scrambling to add, "Sir."

"What's your safe word, Olivia?" Aiden asked from behind her.

"Orchid, Sir."

"Good girl. And if you're not able to speak, I want you to tap three times on Camden's chest. He'll make sure everything stops. Understood?"

"Yes, Sir." She tried to sound polite. She truly did. But the words were dripping with impatience.

Luckily, Camden must've felt the same way. Without another word, he grabbed her hips, lifting her up into position before immediately slamming her down, impaling her on his cock. Her loud cry was echoed by the two women in the pool, who were evidently well into their own fun. Knowing they were getting each other off as they watched made her even wetter.

As promised, Camden fucked her with hard, punishing strokes, controlling her every movement with an ease that left her breathless. Then more hands were on her ass—Aiden's this time. Though it had only been four days, she was sure she'd recognize his touch forever. "Please," she said again, as he tilted her hips up slightly and spread her ass cheeks wide. "*Please*, Sir."

Camden slammed her down one more time, then held her there, his grip tight enough to leave bruises. And then Aiden was pushing through her tight ring, slowly, too slowly, stretching and filling her with such agonizing patience she was almost sure she'd explode.

When at last Aiden was fully sheathed within her, the stream of obscenities that ran through her mind was so foul, Aiden would stop everything to administer a punishment if he heard it. Being fucked while plugged was *absolutely nothing* compared to this. It was the most delicious pain of her fucking life.

Miraculously, she managed to confine herself to only saying, "*Holy shit!*" out loud.

And Jesus fucking Christ in Heaven, now they were moving. They alternated at first, one pushing in while the other pulled out, their rhythm so perfect she was sure they'd done it before. The realization only made her blood run hotter.

Head bent low over Camden's chest, she let them move and position her however they wanted. Let them use her, as if she'd been reduced to nothing but a vessel created solely for their pleasure, with no will of her own. Her whole body trembled with the rush of excitement that brought her.

"Please, may—I come?" she asked, breathing so hard she had to take a break halfway through. God, she was so fucking close.

"Before my cock is even in your mouth?" Mason sounded even sterner than usual, and Olivia knew she must have made a major foursome faux pas. But fucking A, how was she supposed to hold off her orgasm when the image of a third dick thrusting into her mouth was now all she could think of?

"I'm *sorry*," she cried as her first orgasm hit her, shuddering through her in intense waves. Shouts of pleasure from the pool—and a long string of near-gibberish from Tara—followed only seconds behind.

Aiden gave her right ass cheek five swift slaps, even as she continued to clench and spasm around his cock. "Naughty girl." His voice was strained, and she took pleasure in knowing he was probably struggling to hold back his own orgasm. "Mason wasn't going to come in your mouth, but after that brazen little display, I think you owe him an apology."

Before she could get her muddled brain to process that, Mason was beside her. He grabbed her face with both hands, his thumbs digging into her cheekbones, the rest of his fingers gripping hard enough to hurt. "Open," he demanded, turning her face toward him until her neck muscles strained.

Not wanting to insult him further, she opened her mouth as wide as it would go.

"You've clearly misunderstood something," Mason said, pushing his cock slowly into her mouth. "This isn't about your pleasure. It's about ours."

She wished she knew how to relax her throat like all the girls in the books she read. She wanted to show him how sorry she was—give him the pleasure he demanded from her.

Before he hit the back of her throat, he was already retreating, pulling out until only the head remained between her lips. "You're nothing but a new toy for us to play with," Mason said, thrusting back in. It was one of the sexiest things Olivia had ever heard in her life.

Her eyelids fluttered closed as Mason sped up. The other two matched his new pace, and sweet fuck, it was too much at once. Too much sensation in too many places, when she was supposed to be focusing on their pleasure. She tightened her lips around Mason's cock and sucked as hard as she could, trying to be a good girl when all she wanted to do was come again.

"That's it," Mason said, his fingers digging into her hollowed cheeks. "Suck me as hard as you can. That's all you are to us—three tight, warm holes for us to fuck."

She moaned loudly, and that was when Mason finally chose to plunge into the back of her throat, choking her with his cock. Olivia gagged and, for a fleeting moment, started to panic, but he was already pulling away.

Not that her relief lasted for long. As Mason hit the back of her throat again, the other two started fucking her in earnest, losing their careful, orchestrated rhythm. It was so overwhelming she couldn't breathe, couldn't think—and then Camden pressed a finger against her clit. She came so fast and hard she saw fucking stars. Every nerve ending in her body was on edge, hypersensitive to the extreme.

As Mason had reminded her, though, it wasn't about her or her needs. She had to keep being their perfect little fucktoy. If Camden would only stop rubbing her clit, maybe she could concentrate.

But he didn't stop. None of it stopped. All three of them kept fucking and rubbing and prying and clutching, and Jesus fuck, she was going to pass out if it didn't end soon.

"You're going to swallow every single drop," Mason said, pumping faster and faster, his hands jerking against her face, "or I'll put you over my knee." No sooner had he said it than he began sending ropes of come down her throat, holding her face still as she struggled to work her sore muscles, swallowing again and again. When at last he pulled himself free from her, she licked her lips, not wanting to give him any reason for displeasure.

"Bend lower," Aiden ordered as Mason finally let go. "Get your ass in the air for me, Liv."

Without hesitation, Olivia buried her face in Camden's neck, her bound hands trapped between their sweaty bodies. Aiden and Camden were in sync again, fucking her simultaneously, while Camden kept torturing her poor clit, and *fuck fuck fuck*, she couldn't possibly come again.

Except Mason reached in, releasing the nipple clamps at the exact moment Camden pinched her clit, *hard*. The new rush of intense pleasure and pain sent her hurtling over the edge as Aiden and Camden shouted their own pleasure, jerking and pulsing deep inside her.

Olivia wasn't sure if she actually did pass out after all, or if she fell into subspace again. But when next she was aware of her surroundings, she, Aiden, and Camden were in a collapsed heap of intertwined limbs on the chaise. Mason sat on the edge, watching her with a fond little smile, stroking her damp hair off her face.

Aiden raised his head enough to plant a gentle kiss on her sweaty neck. "You were perfect, Liv. Absolutely perfect."

CHAPTER 11
Aiden

How they were already at the end of day five, Aiden had no idea. In all his years at the Manor, a week had never flown by so quickly, and he found himself wishing there was a way to extend Olivia's stay.

But she would be leaving on Saturday morning, whether he wanted her to or not, and his next guest would arrive Sunday afternoon like clockwork.

"Penny for your thoughts?" Olivia said, watching him from the other side of the bed.

"Hmm?" He glanced over at her. Christ, she was beautiful. She was sprawled on top of the duvet, belly down and completely naked. He was sure her luscious ass and thighs hurt too much for any form of contact, as they still bore all his marks.

They'd spent the day down in the dungeon, trying every single thing Liv was interested in. Aiden wanted her to have confidence in herself when she left the Manor and took her next steps into the lifestyle at home. If she knew how all the equipment and furniture worked, and how everything would feel, maybe she wouldn't be too anxious to try again.

She even had a single cane mark across the center of her bottom.

The one had been enough for her, and Aiden had held her for several minutes after she'd shouted her safe word.

"I'm just wondering what has you brooding so sexily," Olivia said with a little smile.

Aiden smoothed his expression. "Nothing for you to worry about," he told her, keeping his tone light. "I was only thinking about how hungry I am, but the kitchen's already closed for the night." It was nearly midnight.

Propping herself up on her elbows, Olivia said, "I'm starving, actually. Want me to go get us a snack?"

"You're such a good girl," Aiden said, brushing her hair out of her face. "Go see what you can find for us. Just make sure you don't make a mess of Gabriel's kitchen, or he'll come after you with a wooden spoon in the morning."

Laughing as if she didn't believe him (on her own sore ass be it), she climbed out of bed and started to dress. She was about to pull a shirt over her head when Aiden ordered, "Stop."

The tank top hung limply from her arms. "What's wrong?"

"Nothing at all," he said, motioning for her to drop her shirt. "You're perfect exactly as you are."

Looking down at her black lace bra and skimpy panties, she seemed confused for a few seconds. Then a glorious blush reddened her skin, and she gave him a shy smile as she dropped her shirt on top of the dresser. "You want me to walk through the house like this, Sir?"

"Mmhmm," he said, rising and crossing the room to her side. Aiden ran a possessive hand over her ass, making her wince at the rough handling. "These marks are too beautiful to cover up. Let everyone see what a naughty girl you are."

Her breathing grew heavier, and she leaned into him, eyes half-closed. "As you wish, Sir."

"Good girl." He bent to capture her mouth with his, kissing her deeply, forcing her to arch her back. Olivia melted against him, her hands quivering against his chest as he plundered her mouth with his tongue. She tasted so damn good, like the red wine and dark chocolate they'd shared a few hours ago. Though it made him long for something sweeter.

Christ, if this went on much longer, he wouldn't be eating anything but her pussy.

Ending the kiss by sheer force of will, Aiden turned her toward the door and gave her ass a gentle pat. Even that was enough to make her hiss. Poor thing. Most of her hurts were easily soothed with some of the cornerstones of aftercare: warm baths and massages, creams and salves, and long nights asleep in the arms of her Dom. But that cane mark might take a week to heal. "Hurry back," he said, "and after we eat, I'll rub some of the numbing cream you love on your bottom."

"Deal," she said, throwing a radiant smile over her shoulder as she hurried out the door. The sight of her—mostly naked, marked from ass to mid-thigh, beaming up at him like he was her whole world—made his heart stop.

Oh, he was so fucked.

He'd fallen for Olivia Adams. Completely, utterly, irrevocably. There was zero point in denying it anymore.

And there wasn't a fucking thing he could do about it. She may have been different from the other women he'd been with—more open, more passionate. Definitely more fragile. But none of that changed the fact she'd come to the Manor for the same reason as the rest of them: because he was a Dom-for-hire. Like his ex from college, it was about the sex and nothing more.

If only Giselle had permanently cured him from catching feelings.

Sighing at his own stupidity, he went to search for the cream, unable to remember where he'd last left it. He'd already given up on the dresser and was digging through the little drawer in his bedside table when a high, shrill scream tore through the quiet house. A second, lower scream came only moments later, and he was one hundred percent sure that one was Olivia.

Aiden slammed through the door and ran as fast as his legs could carry him. And his weren't the only footsteps pounding through the halls. At least two others were sprinting toward the sounds emanating from the kitchen—sounds that now had all the classic hallmarks of a catfight.

"What the fuck is Stacey doing *now*?" Jonathan said, as he and Aiden rounded into the back hall from opposite directions.

Aiden pushed past Jonathan and hurtled through the dining room without responding. If Jonathan's sub had hurt his Olivia, there would be hell to fucking pay.

Relief rushed through Aiden when he finally burst through the kitchen door, finding Rafe with both arms around Stacey, doing his level best to restrain her. Rafe was well more than twice her size, but he clearly had his hands full: she was writhing, flailing, kicking, biting, and anything else she could do to get away, all the while screaming her head off.

Ignoring the little hellcat, Aiden went straight to Olivia. She stood about ten feet from the others, arms wrapped tightly around her stomach, shoulders hunched and head bent low. Her face was hidden behind the curtain of her wild, tousled hair; it was like she'd taken a stroll next to a fucking tornado.

"Liv?" he whispered, gently brushing her hair back and cupping her face with both his hands. She winced and tried to pull away, but he didn't let her. "Let me look."

She wouldn't meet his eyes as he raised her head, staring off toward the walk-in freezer instead. There was a bright red mark across her left cheek where she'd obviously been slapped, and several nasty scratches running from her lower jaw down her neck.

"*Christ*," he muttered, passing his gaze over the rest of her. There were more scratches on her arms and stomach, and the beginning of a hell of a bruise on her left thigh. One strap of her bra hung broken and dejected down her back.

The screaming stopped at long last, and Aiden glanced over. Rafe and Jonathan had finally managed to restrain Stacey. She was still breathing heavily, but no longer had that frantic look in her eyes.

Jonathan looked up, and as soon as their gazes met, Aiden said, "I want her fucking *gone*."

"*Me?*" Stacey shrieked, struggling against their grips again, trying to rip Rafe's hands away. After only a few seconds, she went limp in their arms, settling on glaring at Olivia instead. "That stupid bitch attacked me! Kick her the fuck out!"

Aiden let out a harsh bark of laughter. "You can't possibly think we'd believe you. Not when you've been harassing Olivia all week."

"Harassing her *all week*?" That frantic look was starting to edge back into her eyes. "For fuck's sake, I've barely even seen her! What lies has that cunt been telling you? She's the one who—"

"*Enough!*" Jonathan shouted, and the full force of his Don't-Fuck-With-Me Dom voice was enough to shut anyone up—even a fake sub like Stacey. The fight went out of her so completely that Jonathan let go, and Rafe loosened his arms. With a long-suffering sigh, Jonathan turned to Rafe. "What can you tell us?"

Rafe regarded Stacey with furious gray-green eyes. "By the time I got here, Stacey had Aiden's girl pinned to the floor. She wasn't even fighting back—only guarding her face with her arms while Stacey whaled on her."

Aiden looked at Stacey with a mocking tilt to his brows. "So she attacked first, but then wouldn't even fight back? That's your story?"

"Look at my face!" Stacey screamed, turning her head so everyone had a good view of the shiner swelling her left eye. "She fucking punched me!

Aiden opened his mouth to once again demand Stacey be thrown out—within the hour, if possible. But before he could, a meek voice at his side whispered, "It's true."

His heart skipped a beat. He whipped around to face Olivia again, frowning deeply. "I beg your pardon?"

Tears were making slow, forlorn tracks down Olivia's face. "I did punch her first."

As Aiden stared down at his sweet little sub with his mouth hanging open, Stacey let out a loud, victorious laugh. "See? I fucking told you. I didn't do shit."

"Oh, you did fucking plenty." There was more anger in Jonathan's voice than Aiden had ever heard there before. "Aiden, you handle your sub and I'll deal with mine. Let's get to the bottom of this once and for all and then figure out what the fuck to do."

"Get to the bottom of *what*?" Stacey demanded, her voice rising a whole octave on the final word. "She just told you—*she's* the one who punched *me*. Are you fucking stupid or—"

"I strongly suggest you don't finish that sentence." Jonathan's voice was absolutely fucking deadly.

She didn't finish it. But she did glare at Jonathan with hatred burning in her eyes. "I swear to fucking God, if you so much as touch me, I will sue you for every goddamn penny you have."

The two stared at each other for several tense seconds, neither so much as twitching. Finally, Jonathan said, "Rafe, would you kindly escort Ms. Blackwood to her room so she can gather her things, and then show her to her car? She's decided to end her stay early."

Her mouth dropped open. "It's—it's fucking midnight."

Jonathan had *I fail to see how that's my problem* written so plainly on his face, he might as well have come out and said it. "There's a lovely inn only eight miles from here, in downtown Fairford. Would you like us to call and make you a reservation?"

"Fuck you," Stacey spat. As soon as Rafe released her, she stomped from the room without a backward glance.

With a look of utter annoyance, Rafe followed in her wake, saying, "You owe me," over his shoulder, to no one in particular.

Once their footsteps faded, the silence in the kitchen was absolutely deafening. Aiden stared at Jonathan, while Jonathan stared at the wall, obviously trying to calm himself down and get his thoughts in order. Olivia was still crying quietly at his side.

Christ, what a fucking disaster.

At last Jonathan looked Aiden in the eye and said, "You know the house rules."

"Of course I know them," he snapped. "I helped fucking write them." It had actually been his idea to include a zero-tolerance policy for fighting between the guests. After this week, they'd have to add a zero-tolerance policy for bullying, too.

Jonathan's jaw clenched. "I'll give you half an hour to figure this shit out. If I don't like what I hear when time is up, she needs to leave, too. Understood?"

Aiden wanted to shout that Jonathan could go fuck himself. He wanted to punch that domineering expression off his fucking face. To carry Liv up to their room, lock the door, and never open it again.

But Jonathan had the final say on everything that went on in the Manor. He always had.

Shoulders rigid and hands fisted at his sides, Aiden nodded. "Understood."

Pinching the bridge of his nose, Jonathan muttered, "I'm getting a fucking headache," and strode from the room.

Aiden watched the kitchen door swing back and forth on its two-way hinges. When at last it stilled, he heaved a deep sigh and forced himself to face Olivia. "Why?"

"I don't know."

"Bullshit." He tried not to feel guilty when she winced at the anger in his voice. There was no way he could accept a total copout answer like that—especially not with Jonathan breathing down his neck. "This isn't a request, Olivia. You heard what Jonathan said. I need answers."

She blinked, and two more tears made slow trails down to her chin. "I don't know what to tell you."

Christ, this was getting him nowhere. Biting back an angry retort, he instead tried to come at it from a different angle. "Unless I'm very mistaken, you've never punched anyone in your entire life." At his expectant look, Olivia shook her head. "Answer me verbally."

Hugging herself even tighter, she whispered, "No, Sir, I've never hit anyone before."

"So why her? Why now? She's been trying to goad you all week, and you've managed to stay perfectly behaved. What happened this time to make it different?"

She gave the tiniest of shrugs and refused to say another word.

"Fine. We'll do things your way." Running a frustrated hand through his hair, he started toward the door. "Olivia, come."

CHAPTER 12
Olivia

F*uck.*

That had been so goddamn stupid. She should've ignored that jealous asshole, grabbed the first edible thing she saw, and gone up to her sexy Dom. She'd be in bed right now, kneeling beside him as he fed her tiny bites, living her fucking dream.

Instead, she would be thrown out in half an hour. There was no doubt in her mind.

She'd never see Aiden again, and would spend the rest of her life wondering what could've been if she'd just walked the fuck away.

And for what? Why had she let Stacey get to her like that? She hadn't been lying to Aiden . . . she genuinely didn't know. She'd been trying to ignore her like the good girl she wanted to be, when all of a sudden, she saw red. Next thing she knew, her hand hurt like a mother-fucker, and Stacey was slapping and scratching and screaming.

Olivia glanced at her right hand. It was swollen as all hell, the skin split on the first two knuckles.

Fuck, fuck, fuck.

She followed Aiden forlornly up the stairs and to their suite, not daring to say a single word in her defense. What could she possibly say?

As soon as the door was shut behind them, Aiden stripped her down, removing her damaged lingerie coldly and efficiently. Then he led her over to the couch, jerked her down over his lap, and started spanking.

No warmup, no breaks. Not so much as a single word. Nothing but constant, hard slaps, one cheek after the other, over and over and over until she was reduced to nothing but the pain.

Olivia didn't try to fight him. She simply buried her face in the couch cushion and sobbed, knowing she deserved every single stroke and so much more.

When he finally stilled, he waited patiently for her to get herself under control, his hand resting on her inner thigh. It was several minutes before she could stop the sobs ripping through her entire body, though she tried desperately to be quiet for him the entire time.

At last, silence fell over the room like a heavy, smothering blanket. Aiden stood, lifting her with him and setting her on her feet. "Come," he said again, leading her around the edge of the couch until she stood facing its arm. "Don't move."

The disappointment and fury in his voice were even worse than the spanking had been. She had to fight the urge to start crying again.

Aiden rummaged around in the dresser drawers for about a minute, and though Olivia longed to see what he was getting, she obediently kept her eyes straight ahead. Nothing in the world could make her disobey him in that moment.

"Hands behind your back," Aiden ordered upon his return. Though his voice was hard, his hands were gentle as he buckled her wrists into wide cuffs, the lining soft against her skin. She gave zero resistance as he pushed her over the arm of the couch, until her forehead rested against the cushion and her already-flaming ass was in perfect position for more punishment.

She squirmed around a bit, trying to ease some of the pressure on her stomach, until Aiden gave her a sharp smack to both sit spots. "Be still. And spread your legs."

Holding in more tears, she did as she was ordered. He buckled her left ankle into another cuff, then did the same with her right. There were several clicks, her legs forced wider apart with each one; he'd attached an adjustable spreader bar to the ankle cuffs. She was stretched so wide, her toes barely reached the floor.

"I'm going to ask you some questions now." He rested a hand firmly against her hip, pressing her down into the couch arm. "And if I don't like the answers . . . well, let's see if I can do anything to motivate you to try harder. What's your safe word?"

"O-orchid, Sir."

"Do *not* forget you can use it." There was a real urgency in his voice, bordering on desperation. "This is a punishment, and it's going to hurt. But at no point are you giving up total control to me. You say that word, everything stops, same as every other time. Do you understand me?"

Olivia held back a whimper. "Yes, Sir." She could hardly even hear her own words.

"Good." He let out a long, slow breath. "Then let's get started. Why did you punch Stacey in the eye?"

"I already told you," she said, knowing he wouldn't believe her, gritting her teeth against the punishment to come. "I don't know."

A wide leather strap came down hard across her ass, once, twice, three times. Olivia let out a yelp of pain at the first, which snapped along the full length of the cane mark, but managed to take the other two without a sound.

"What did she say to you?"

"She said all the same stuff as before, about me being fat and ugly, and how she can't believe anyone would ever fuck me." Olivia thought back to the scene in the kitchen again, and for one fleeting moment, she actually smiled. "I told her I'd fucked three of the five Doms here, so I was pretty sure that put me one up on her."

Aiden was quiet for several seconds, and she suspected he was suppressing a laugh. She sure hoped so—she'd be proud of that comeback until her dying day.

At last, he spoke in a completely neutral tone: "What happened after that?"

"That's when she got *really* nasty."

When she didn't continue, Aiden brought down the strap three more times, even harder than before and right on her sit spots. The leather even wrapped around her hip, and she couldn't help crying out again.

Desperate to avoid his strap at all costs, Olivia listed off some of the worst comments Stacey had made about her body, her sexual inexperience, her intelligence. There was no cohesion to her retelling—words simply bubbled out of her in whatever order they came to mind.

"Enough," Aiden said at last. "I get the picture. But how is that any different from what she said before?"

"I don't know." She couldn't put her finger on *what* made it different, but damnit, it had sure fucking felt different to her. Without a reason, though, all she could say was, "I guess it's not?"

An exasperated sigh. "Then why did you punch her?"

"I just . . . did."

That time, Aiden brought the strap up between her legs. The supple leather snapped against her pussy and clit, making her scream with the pain, and Jesus fucking Christ, she was literally going to die. She tried to clamp her legs together before he could do it again, but she'd forgotten about the fucking spreader bar. All she managed to do was bruise her own ankles with the cuffs as the strap hit her again.

Bitch. Fat. Ugly. Stupid. Boring.

Highlights of Stacey's insults flashed through her mind, playing on repeat as Aiden continued to punish her most sensitive flesh.

And then new ones Stacey didn't even say started piling on. But they were in the same tone, delivered with the same hateful, condescending sneer.

Useless. Lazy. Loser. Embarrassment. Pointless.

Mistake.

"I'm not a fucking mistake!" Olivia shouted it at the top of her lungs.

Aiden had been raising the strap again, but his arm fell to his side with a soft *thud* when she spoke. "What did you say?"

Tears were pouring down her face as she forced out, "I am *not* a fucking *mistake*."

He seemed genuinely taken aback when he said, "I never said you were."

Goddamnit, she was messing everything up again, and now she was crying too hard to explain, and what the actual fuck was Aiden supposed to do with a weird-ass statement like that? If she wasn't out on her ass in the parking lot in the next five minutes, she'd be the luckiest person in the entire world.

"*Please!*" she wailed, desperate for him to understand, unable to get anything else out. She was starting to hyperventilate again, her mind such a whirlwind of panic and anguished memory that she could barely think.

"Did . . ." He seemed uncertain of what to say or do. "Did your father tell you you're a mistake?"

She couldn't answer with words. All she could do was cry even harder. But that was enough.

"Oh, Liv." He had her out of the cuffs and spreader bar in seconds flat, then pulled her upright. "I've got you." Scooping her up, he carried her over to a chair, settling down with her in his lap. "I've got you. I've got you." He said it again and again in his gentlest, most soothing voice, as he held her tight and safe against his chest.

God, it felt so good. If only she could stay within the shelter of his arms forever.

But her life wasn't a fucking fairy tale.

Olivia sniffed, then looked around for a box of tissues with no luck. She'd always been an ugly crier, with lots of snot and phlegm and all the gross shit. And here she was, without even a sleeve to wipe her nose on. "I'm sorry," she said, her voice low and hoarse.

Aiden wrapped his arms around her even tighter. "No. You're not going to apologize. Not for this."

"But your boss—"

"Jonathan isn't my boss. He's my business partner." With a frustrated little sound, he added, "He's technically the senior partner, which is why he has final say on some things. But this is every bit as much my business as it is his. I practically built the fucking place. And I'm not letting him railroad me on this."

For the life of her, she couldn't understand why he'd go out on a limb for her like that. No one had ever thought she was worth much effort before. Of course, she'd never let anyone in as much as Aiden before. Even he was merely standing in the doorway to all her fucked-uppery, getting only the smallest glimpse.

"I want—" She paused for several seconds, lost in her jumble of anxious thoughts. "I want to explain some things. About my childhood. My dad. I . . . I think you deserve to know."

Aiden kissed the top of her head. "Only tell me what you genuinely want me to know. No one *deserves* your pain. You don't owe it to me or anyone else, and you never will, do you understand?"

Blinking back fresh tears, Olivia almost asked, *Why did you have to be so perfect?* It wasn't fucking fair. How was it she'd finally found the most amazing man on the planet, and she only got to keep him for a week?

"I understand," she said instead.

"Good girl." He kissed her hair again, and she closed her eyes, letting his warmth seep into her. "Take your time."

Keeping her eyes closed, she took several slow, calming breaths. She could fucking do this. "I grew up poor. *Really* poor. And my dad always had a million and one reasons for why it wasn't his fault. If he lost his job, it wasn't because he was a lazy asshole who no one liked being around. It was cause someone else *obviously* fucked him over. Someone who saw how great and wonderful and smart he was, and felt threatened, and had to get rid of him."

"I know the type," Aiden said, running his fingertips softly up and down her arm. "I assume this happened often?"

"Constantly. And then if he couldn't afford something, or we got evicted again, it wasn't because he'd lost his job for the hundredth time, and he'd spent whatever money he did have on booze, or fucked it away on stupid shit we didn't need. It was always because of *me*."

His hand stilled for a moment, then resumed its oh-so-gentle up and down, up and down. "You were the easiest target."

She shrugged. She'd certainly been the smallest and weakest, so it made a lot of sense.

"Where was your mom in all this?"

"She was there. Drunk most of the time. She used to get this weird, vague look in her eyes when he was going after me. Like she'd completely checked out."

Aiden wrapped his arms around her again, holding her close. "I'm sorry your mom wasn't willing to protect you."

"She was probably glad it was me instead of her." There was more fire in her voice than she'd intended. "And the part that really fucks me up is, I almost can't even bring myself to blame her. Jesus, he could be so cruel." His voice was still in her head, as clear as it had been fifteen years ago. "'Everything would be better if you'd never been born. I wouldn't be married to this fucking useless slut. I wouldn't be stuck in this piece of shit town. Having you was the biggest fucking mistake of my life. I should've made her go through with the abortion.'"

"Christ," Aiden said, the word dripping with venom.

"He's the reason I'm always so afraid of making mistakes," she admitted, wanting him to finally understand her extreme anxiety. "I wasn't ever allowed to mess up when I was a kid. Every little thing I did wrong meant I was a stupid, lazy fuck-up. No matter how hard I tried, he always found something to yell at me about, even if he had to make it up."

"If he's still alive, I'll beat the ever-loving shit out of him."

"I don't know if he is or not," she said honestly, smiling a little at his threat. "I left the day I turned eighteen, and I never once looked back. And they don't seem to have ever tried to find me, thank God."

"Where did you go?"

"I stayed with a friend and her parents until I finished high school, and then moved to Austin in the fall. I wanted to be an accountant, and maybe even study to be a CPA someday. It was the most boring, stable thing I could think of, and I knew if I could do that, I'd never be anything like my parents. I'd always be able to find a job, and always make good money. That security—it was literally everything to me at the time. And I got a full academic scholarship for undergrad at the University of Texas."

Aiden sounded proud as all hell when he said, "My brilliant girl."

Tears sprang to her eyes again. No one had ever been proud of her before. "I had to apply in secret. My dad fucking *hated* that I was smarter than him. He'd always go on about what a useless loser I was, and how high and mighty I was thinking I was so smart, when he had more intelligence in one finger than I had in my whole body. Every time

I knew something he didn't, or he saw my grades . . . hell, reading a book could set him off."

"Sounds like a classic narcissist to me."

She took a moment to consider it. "That makes a lot of sense. He definitely did think he was smarter than everyone else, no matter how much evidence there was to the contrary. But one night, he got drunk and made me take an IQ test he took online. I think he wanted to rub it in how much higher his score was than mine."

"I assume you kicked his ass?"

She grinned. "You fucking know it." But her smile slipped away after mere seconds. "He was so mad. It must've completely fucked with his view of himself. That's one of the only times he ever hit me."

"I'm so sorry, Liv." Aiden sounded like his heart was breaking. "He was a small man who wanted the people around him to feel even smaller than he did."

Aiden was right. She knew he was. But something else was lurking in the back of her mind—had been lurking there for years. If she was being completely honest with herself, that niggling thought was part of what had kept her out of the lifestyle for so long.

"Isn't it a little fucked up though?" she asked tentatively.

"It's majorly fucked up."

She shook her head. "No, I mean me."

"I . . . don't know what you mean." She could hear the frown in his voice.

Olivia took several seconds to think about what she wanted to say, knowing she'd only get one chance to get it right. "I spent my whole childhood under the control of someone else. Someone who used that control to hurt me so much I might never fully recover. So how the hell did I end up like this? BDSM should *repulse* me, shouldn't it? Yet here I am, begging to be spanked and ordered around and fucked like I'm your toy. How did those wires get so fucking twisted in my brain?" She let out something halfway between a sigh and a groan. "Fuck, I need so much therapy."

"Oh, my sweet girl." Aiden shifted her around in his lap so they were face to face, her legs straddling his. "What we're doing together is *nothing* like what happened with your father. He was an abuser, plain and simple. Everything we do is one-hundred percent consensual."

"I know, but I'm consenting to be *hurt*."

He brushed her hair out of her eyes, gently cupping her face. "Did the way your father treated you ever make you happy?"

"*Fuck* no." She was horrified by the very idea.

Pressing their foreheads together, Aiden whispered, "What about what I do to you?"

Olivia closed her eyes, leaning into him even more, desperate to be as close as possible when she admitted, "I've never been happier in my life."

"Nothing got twisted in your brain, Liv. I promise." He brushed his lips against the top of her head. "You were born a submissive, not made one. It was always there inside you, waiting for you to discover it, just like I was always going to be a Dom."

She frowned, rolling that idea around in her head. "How can you be sure?"

"Remember how I said my parents disowned me? How they're ultra-religious and conservative? If being raised by them was going to turn me into something, it sure as fuck wouldn't be *this*." His voice grew almost regretful as he admitted, "For a long time, I wished I could make myself different. For them. To make them accept me again. But I can't change who I am, and neither can you."

"But my dad—"

"Wasn't a thing like us," Aiden insisted. "He's an abusive piece of shit, nothing more. When you're with me, or any other Dom worth a damn, you have all the power. You can bring everything to a complete stop with a single word. Don't you ever forget that. And a real Dom doesn't see your submission as something to make himself more powerful or important. I see it as a gift. The greatest fucking gift in the world."

It felt like the weight of an elephant had been lifted from her chest. "Aiden," she said, knowing she needed to tell him how she felt about him, that it was now or never. "I—"

Three sharp knocks on the door shattered the moment into a thousand jagged pieces.

"Fuck," Aiden and Olivia said, in perfect unison.

They looked at each other, surprise all over both their faces. Then Aiden chuckled. "All right, my wonderful, naughty girl. I guess I'd better go calm Jonathan down. How much of this do I have your permission to tell him?"

Olivia frowned as she thought about it. "I trust you completely. Do whatever you need to so I can stay here with you."

Giving her a slow, sweet kiss on the lips, Aiden said, "You can't possibly know what your trust means to me."

Jonathan knocked again before calling, "I'm starting to lose my patience," through the door.

"I'll be right out," Aiden called back, then helped her stand. "I don't know how long I'll be. Why don't you get into bed and try to rest while I'm gone? You've had one hell of a day."

She certainly had. Grateful for the suggestion, Olivia crossed the room and flopped facedown on top of the duvet, burying her head in one of the ultra-soft pillows.

"Christ, you're beautiful," Aiden said, running a single finger down the center of her spine. Goosebumps popped up all over her skin. "I'll be back as soon as I can. I promise." With a parting kiss to her temple, he joined Jonathan out in the hall. Their voices were a low murmur as they walked away.

Jonathan had better fucking let her stay. Once he understood, he had to.

Didn't he?

If Aiden couldn't convince him, maybe she could. All she needed was to come up with the exact right thing to say to *make* him understand. If he truly knew how Stacey had made her feel—like she was back in her parents' house, trapped in the one place she swore she'd never be again—he'd have to forgive her.

She must've drifted off while she planned and schemed, because next thing she knew, Aiden was gently shaking her awake.

"Jonathan is in the hall," he said, helping her sit up. "He wants to talk to you."

Olivia studied him as she got to her feet, searching for some clue of what was to come. But his face was like a perfect mask, and she was too afraid to ask.

"Here," Aiden said, helping her slip into a short satin robe. Even the smooth fabric burned against the marks on her ass and thighs, but she was grateful for it anyway. This wasn't a conversation she wanted to have naked.

She made it to the end of the bed, but her feet would take her no farther. Aiden seemed to understand, for he let Jonathan into the room rather than try to force her the rest of the way to the door.

When Jonathan entered, his expression was as unreadable as her Dom's. Fucking fuck, was she seriously getting thrown out? She fisted her hands in the robe, crushing the thin fabric between her fingers.

"Thank you, Olivia," Jonathan said after a strained silence.

Her brows shot up. "For what?"

"For trusting Aiden with your story. And for allowing him to trust me with it in turn. I understand what happened now. I know that couldn't have been easy, and I'm deeply impressed with how strong you've been through this ordeal."

All the tension went out of Olivia's shoulders. He was going to let her stay.

"However," Jonathan continued, before she could get too excited, "I assume this isn't a story you want anyone else to know."

He didn't phrase it as a question, but was clearly waiting for her to respond. "No. I've never actually told anyone about all this before tonight." Not even her five therapists. Which probably explained why none of them had ever been much help, come to think of it.

"Aiden thought as much." Sighing, he rubbed the bridge of his nose. "Unfortunately, all six partners have agreed that, for the sake of maintaining the Manor's stellar reputation, we can't let you stay here after evicting the person you attacked. Not when we can't give an explanation of why. We even got our silent partner on the phone, to get a more"—he pondered his word choice for a moment—"*neutral* opinion."

Olivia's gaze flew to Aiden's, accusation in her eyes. "You *agreed* to this?" The fucker didn't even have the good grace to look guilty. He stood there with no expression at all, still as a statue. Turning her glare onto Jonathan, she spat, "You gonna make me a reservation at the inn eight miles away? Or do I not get that courtesy since I swung first?"

A hard Dom look stole into his eyes. "That's quite enough. You aren't being kicked out, Olivia. Not necessarily."

"I—what? I'm not?"

"We're not finished, Liv," Aiden said, his mask finally slipping. There was desperation etched into every line in his forehead, into the downward tilt of his mouth. "Not even fucking close. You remember how I told you about my cabin?"

Heart in her throat, she nodded. *Oh God, please mean what I think you mean!*

"Aiden's willing to open his cabin to you for the rest of your stay. Normally, we obviously wouldn't take our guests off Manor property." Jonathan gave a little shrug. "But, given the circumstances, I have no objection to this arrangement, as long as you're comfortable with it."

Before she even knew she was moving, Olivia had flown across the room and into Aiden's arms. Burying his nose in her hair, he wrapped his arms tightly around her, holding her close.

Jonathan chuckled, his stoic veneer cracking for the first time since she'd met him. "I guess I know your answer."

"Thank you," Olivia said, to either of them, or both. What did it matter, so long as she got to stay with Aiden? "Thank you for understanding."

Looking over the top of her head, Aiden promised, "We'll leave as soon as the sun comes up."

CHAPTER 13
Aiden

Early morning sunlight fought its way through the canopy, giving the road to Aiden's cabin a dappled look. The shadows also played across Olivia's face as she slept in the passenger seat of his Land Rover, head leaning against the window. Her mouth hung open, and a tiny rivulet of drool fell from one corner of her lips.

Christ, she was cute.

"Liv," he said, giving her leg a gentle shake.

She shifted in her seat and made a noise that sounded like, "*Huuurng.*"

Shoulders shaking with a silent laugh, he nudged her leg a little harder. "It's time to wake up, Liv. We're almost there."

Her eyes still didn't open, but she did shut her mouth, swiping the wetness from her chin with the back of her hand. "Okay, okay," she said, rolling her head back and forth to ease the crick in her neck. "I'm awake."

Just in time, too. Aiden rounded the last turn in his road (more of an extremely long private driveway, really), and stopped the car well back from the house. He wanted her to get the best possible view. He was surprised by the nervous pounding in his chest. He'd never cared what anyone thought about his cabin before. Hell, he'd never even *shown* it to anyone before, not so much as a picture. "What do you think?"

Olivia slowly blinked her eyes open, quite obviously still half asleep. When her gaze lit upon the cabin, however, her eyes grew round and her breath caught in her chest. "Oh, wow," she breathed after a few moments. "Aiden, it's *gorgeous.*"

Aiden glowed with pride. He was no architect, of course, so he couldn't take total credit. But he'd handpicked every single aspect of his little hideaway, and done a good deal of the work himself, until it felt like an extension of his soul. It might as well have a sign hanging over the front door that said, "AIDEN MCLAREN, IF HE WAS A HOUSE."

He watched Olivia as her gaze took in the multi-colored stone façade, the metal roof with its two gables, the garden of wildflowers out front, and the large, covered porch wrapping around three sides of the house. Trees surrounded everything, for he'd only had the heart to cut down the bare minimum of the ancient oaks, birches, and pines. He'd tried to create a forest paradise, and from the awe on Olivia's face, he'd succeeded. And she hadn't even seen the real showstopper yet.

"Come on," he said, driving up to the front of the house. "I want to show you the rest."

She was out of the car before he even turned it off, following the stone pathway through the wildflower garden. The riot of colors surrounding her, her golden yellow sundress, and the way her black curls tumbled wildly down her back combined to create an image so beautiful, Aiden couldn't help pulling out his phone and snapping a picture. If they were only to spend one more day together, Aiden wanted to remember it for the rest of his life.

Leaving their bags in the car, he moved up beside her, putting a possessive hand on her hip. He had a whole duffle bag full of fun things for them to play with later, but for now, all he needed was Liv—and perhaps the single item he'd slipped into his pocket as they left their suite an hour ago.

"I can hear running water," she said, glancing around for its source. "Is there a river nearby?"

"You'll see in a moment," he promised, leading her up the steps to the front door. Unlocking it, he pushed the door open and motioned for her to precede him into the house.

With an excited glint in her eyes, Olivia practically skipped over the threshold. "Holy shit!" she exclaimed, hurrying across the enormous room that made up almost the whole interior of the house. She got so close to the floor-to-ceiling windows forming the entire back wall that her breath fogged the glass. "Oh my God, *Aiden*. I've never seen anything more beautiful."

Moving up behind her at a more sedate pace, he put his hands on her shoulders. "I spent months trying to find the perfect piece of land," he said, voice soft as he gazed outside. "As soon as I saw this spot, I knew. This was where I wanted my home to be for the rest of my life."

The house was built at the edge of a stone bluff, and a wide, gentle creek wound its way by about fifteen feet below. The morning sun sparkled against the water, making it shine like thousands of perfect diamonds.

"Thank you for bringing me here," Olivia said, leaning back against him. "I know this is where you go when you want to be alone. I can't tell you what it means to me that you wanted me here with you."

"I told you," Aiden said, pushing slowly but insistently forward until her breasts and hips were pressed up against the window. "We're not done yet."

Bracing herself against the thick glass with her palms, she arched her hips back toward him. "No, we're not," she agreed, her breath hitching as he lifted the skirt of her dress.

Aiden thrust his own hips forward, until the erection straining against his zipper was pressed tightly against her ass. "Hands up here," he said, sliding them up to either side of her face. "Don't move. Your poor ass can't take much more punishment right now."

She whimpered. "Yes, Sir."

"I'm going to give you a choice," he said, reaching down and gripping her scant panties in his fist. "I can fuck your pussy or your ass. But I want you to ask me nicely for what you want. And if you're a very good girl and do exactly as you're told, I'll allow you to come."

Olivia's hands clenched convulsively against the window, but she managed to keep them where he wanted them. "My ass, please, Sir," she said, already breathing heavily.

"Oh, you're going to have to do better than that." Aiden tugged sharply on her panties, tearing them from her body with the sound of ripping fabric. He fucking loved her squeak of surprise, and loved even more that she remained in position. "I know how much you love a good ass fucking, Liv. Tell me how much you want it."

Pushing her now-naked ass back against him, she begged, "Please fuck me in the ass, Sir. Nothing in the world makes me feel better than your cock in my ass, fucking me as hard as you can. You know what an anal slut I am."

"Mmm." He grasped her hips and held her against him even tighter, relishing the feel of her against the bulge in his jeans. "Such pretty words from my good girl."

She moved her hips in a tiny circle, the little minx, and he had to bite back a groan. "Stay," he ordered, stepping away to undo his pants. He pushed them down his hips only enough for his cock to spring free, then fished the tiny individual packet of lubricant from his pocket.

"Please," Olivia moaned when he tore the packet open, wiggling her ass at him in invitation.

"Patience," he scolded with a dark chuckle. He pushed two fingers slowly into her, pumping them in and out to spread the lube around. "Is this what you want?"

She groaned. "It's not enough, Sir." Her voice shook with lust and excitement. "I need your cock inside me. *Please.* I'll die if I have to wait any more." Despite her words, she pushed back against his fingers hungrily, taking them into her as deep as they could go, and cried out when he removed them.

Christ, he loved it when she begged. Spreading her ass cheeks wide, he pressed the head of his cock up against her tight entrance. "All right, my beautiful little anal slut. Open up for me."

Her whole body vibrated at his words, and she panted heavily as he pushed his way through her tight ring of muscle. "*Fuuuuuuuuck,*" she said, more a moan than actual speech.

He pulled out halfway, and then slammed back in, flattening her completely against the window. A slight sheen of sweat covered her skin, making her arms slippery against the glass.

"*More.*" She was pleading again, which sent a jolt straight through his cock. "Please, please, please, pl—" Her words fell away as he started to fuck her properly, replaced by harsh, jagged breaths.

"Your ass is mine," he growled into her ear, pumping in and out of her as hard as he could. "Your pussy is mine. Your mouth is mine. This" —he snaked his hand around her hip, forcing his way between her and the glass, fingers searching until he found her clit—"is *mine.*"

She gave a sharp cry of pleasure that ended in something almost like a sob. "I'm yours." She sounded absolutely nothing like herself, voice high and breathless. "All of me. Take whatever you want."

Fucking hell, he'd never heard anything sexier in his entire life. He almost came right then and there, but managed to get ahold of himself at the last second. He'd make sure to push her over the edge first if it fucking killed him.

Wrapping one hand up in her long tangle of hair, he pulled hard, arching her neck back. "Fucking fuck!" Her hips bucked out of control, losing their rhythm as he applied more pressure to her clit.

"Fly for me, love," he rasped out, and she screamed her pleasure, spasmodically clenching around his cock.

Christ almighty, her ass was like a fucking vise, and he couldn't have held back any longer if he'd tried. His shouts joined hers as he came *hard*, and he completely flattened her against the window with his body, his hands covering hers.

It wasn't until they'd both stilled, their panting breaths slowing back to normal, that he realized he'd called her *love* instead of *Liv*. It was more than possible she'd been too far-gone to notice. Given their looming parting, that certainly seemed like the best possible outcome.

So why was he desperately hoping she'd heard him?

CHAPTER 14
Olivia

L*ove.*
    Had he actually called her that? Or had she heard him wrong?
There was no way. She'd been panting and moaning and screaming like a fucking porn star at the time. It was much easier to believe he said Liv and she misheard him, than that he was all of a sudden using the L-word with her.

Right?

Sweet Christ, she literally had no idea. And because there was no way to find out without straight-up asking him (not a fucking chance), she was lost inside her head, spiraling out of control instead. She'd been so distracted during the bit of bondage they were experimenting with an hour ago, Aiden had called it quits and stalked off to cook dinner.

Which meant she was letting one potentially misheard word fuck up her last day with Aiden. And there was no way she could let that keep happening. Not unless she wanted to regret it for the rest of her life.

"Dinner's ready," Aiden said, voice devoid of any emotion.

She watched him leave the galley kitchen, a plate in each hand, from her spot in an overstuffed armchair by the back window-wall. It was easy to see him from the opposite side of the house, for with the exception of the single bathroom, the whole cabin was a giant open-concept room.

There was the kitchen with cabinets in a light, knotty wood and gray-green granite countertops. The main sitting area clustered around the large woodburning fireplace, with red leather couch and chairs, and a plush, gray-and-white rug. A spiral staircase up to a loft, holding his king-size bed and built-in bookcases full to bursting. And of course, the single chair where she sat, tucked into the corner by the window, two additional bookcases against the wall behind her.

Aiden set the plates on the breakfast bar and gave her an uncertain look. As if he wasn't sure she even wanted to dine with him. As confused and unfocused as she'd been, she couldn't blame him.

Goddamnit, she'd royally fucked things up.

A plan quickly forming in her head, she tried to rise from the chair in one fluid, lithe movement. Unfortunately, those two words had never been associated with her before, and that sure wasn't changing now. Not with the way she lurched out of the chair like Frankenstein's fucking monster.

Fighting back an embarrassed grimace, she tried to walk across the room in a sexy, seductive way, swaying her hips, looking up at him through her eyelashes. It was hard to tell from his expression whether it was working. His only indication he noticed anything different was a slight lift of a single eyebrow.

I can do this, she told herself, redoubling her efforts. What if he thought she was getting bored with him? Or perhaps that she'd already emotionally shut down, since she was leaving in the morning. She had to do whatever she could to show him he was everything to her—

A plan that fell completely to pieces when she ran into the sofa and toppled sideways.

"Oh, for fuck's sake," she muttered as she hit the floor. Giving up completely, she stayed on the ground, covering her eyes with her hands.

The floor vibrated beneath her as Aiden's footsteps thundered across the room. "Are you okay?" She didn't have to look at him to know he was struggling not to laugh. It was obvious as all hell.

"I'm fine," she said, groaning, certain she was blushing from head to toe. "Go eat your dinner and leave me to die in peace."

Losing his battle with politeness at last, he laughed out loud. "You're not going to die," he said, still chuckling as he pried her hands away from her face. "Come on. Let me get a look at you." Despite her struggles and objections, he hauled her to her feet, holding her out in front of him at arm's length. He turned her this way and that, making a show of checking her for injuries, her blush deepening all the while. "There doesn't appear to be any permanent damage."

Yeah, not to her body. Her ego was well and truly eviscerated, though.

"All right, you ridiculous creature," he said, tucking two fingers under her chin and gently lifting until she finally looked at him. "Why don't you tell me what on earth that was?"

She mumbled her answer, too mortified to speak at a volume humans could hear.

"Want to try that again in English?" he said, one corner of his mouth quirking up.

Knowing it was a lost cause, she screwed her eyes shut and blurted, "I was trying to be sexy for you, okay?" Aaaand now she was crying. Good lord, could this get any more embarrassing? "And apparently I suck at it, because even before I collided with the furniture, you obviously had no idea what I was doing. So yay me."

"Oh, Liv." He gathered her to his chest, resting his chin against the top of her head. "I'm sorry. I know I shouldn't tease you. It's just, you're the sexiest woman I've ever met in my life. You're the only thing I've thought about from the moment I started reading your application six months ago. And then when I finally saw you in person . . . fuck me, I was done for. You have to know that by now."

Breathing in the subtle scent of his cologne, she forced some of the tension out of her body. "I'm sorry," she said, wrapping her arms around his waist. "I know I'm screwing everything up. I was trying to fix it, but I screwed that up, too."

"You're not screwing anything up." He sounded like he genuinely meant it, though she couldn't imagine how. "This is a hard night for both of us."

Olivia pulled away, looking up into his eyes. "Is it really?" She was almost afraid to hear his answer.

Frowning, he asked, "Is it really what?"

"Hard for both of us."

Hurt flashed through his gorgeous brown eyes, there one second and hidden the next. If she'd blinked, she would've missed it. "I'm not sure what you mean," he said, voice now neutral.

Fuck. She hadn't meant to hurt his feelings. But she *needed* to know the truth. What was real, and what was merely part of his act? This was his job, after all. If they met again someday, would he be stiffly telling her he didn't feel the same connection she did, like he'd told Stacey? Or was it possible that maybe, just maybe, this all meant as much to him as it did to her?

"You must've done this dozens of times," she said, talking a little too fast, her heart pounding against her ribs. "I figured maybe you were used to it by now? The goodbye part, I mean."

His lips formed a silent O. Reaching up, he cupped her face between his hands. "It's never been difficult before. This is the first time I haven't wanted the week to end." And then he was kissing her. Slowly at first, his soft lips so gentle against hers, his stubble only brushing faintly against her skin.

Olivia didn't know who deepened the kiss, him or her. All she knew was they were suddenly clinging to one another, mouths moving frantically, clothes being shoved out of the way.

Dinner completely forgotten, he lifted her so she was perched on the back of the couch, her legs circling his waist, arms wrapped around his neck. "Please don't be gentle," Olivia said, digging her heels into his firm ass, forcing him closer to her.

Aiden began to fuck her with long, intense strokes, the thumb of one hand gently brushing over her clit, teasing her, driving her wild. The back of the couch was hard and unforgiving beneath her, digging into her bruised and tortured flesh without reprieve. When Aiden slid his free hand down, gripping her ass possessively, the dual sensations were a sweet ecstasy of pain.

"Don't cry, Liv."

Good lord, she hadn't even realized she was. It was all too much. The dwindling countdown in her head was like the constant *tick-tock, tick-tock* of a timer on a bomb, making it impossible to forget the end was coming. How could she lose herself in this sweet, agonizing fuck—

possibly the last they ever shared—when her whole world was about to implode?

Clutching him as tightly as she could, Olivia buried her face in his neck and tried to focus on the pain and pleasure coursing through her body. If she never felt like this again for the rest of her life, at least she'd be able to lose herself in the memory.

Though if she truly never felt like this again, it might be easier to forget.

Hours later, they lay in bed together, Olivia's head on his shoulder, her whole body tucked up against his side. He'd been lazily running his fingertips up and down her arm for at least twenty minutes, neither of them saying a word.

Part of her was afraid to break the silence. It was so perfect and peaceful. But there was something she needed to say, and she'd never have the nerve to get it out in the light of day.

"Thank you."

His hand stilled. "For what?"

"For understanding me. For fixing me."

Aiden gave her arm a gentle squeeze. "You didn't need to be fixed, Liv."

"My life was empty before. All I did was work and dream about stuff I was too afraid to do." She took a deep breath and forced herself to continue. "I'm thirty-three years old, and don't think I've ever really been happy before I came here. That sounds pretty damn broken to me."

He held her closer, not saying a word.

"But now . . . maybe I don't have to be alone. Maybe everything will be different, all because of you."

"You're the one who filled out the application," Aiden said, his voice soft as a caress. "Without that, I never would've known you exist. So it seems to me everything will be different now because of *you*—because you took control of your own life and made it happen. And I'm so fucking proud of you for finding the strength to do that."

Could that really be true? Had she made this happen herself?

I love you. I love you. Just say the words: I. Love. You.

But she couldn't do it. How fucking unhinged would he think she was for declaring her love when they'd only known each other for six days? And how pathetic did it make her that she'd paid someone to dominate her (no matter what Aiden said about *consenting adults*), and then fell for him—as if their entire "relationship" wasn't one big transaction?

His rejection now, in the middle of the night and an hour away from her car, would be the most unbearably painful and mortifying moment of her life.

Letting him go without even trying, though . . . that was even worse.

Screwing her eyes up tight, she forced out, "I know I got myself banned from the Manor. But is this really it? I drive away tomorrow, and we never see each other again?"

"Do you want to see me again?" The words were almost robotic.

Christ almighty, she was exactly like Stacey. Imagining a connection that wasn't really there. Doing her best to sound flirty instead of heartbroken, she said, "Well, you have to admit, it's like fireworks on the Fourth of July when we fuck."

He chuckled, sliding a hand along her cheekbone and up into her hair. "Ain't that a fucking fact."

"Is it like that with most of your other subs?" What a pitiful thing to ask—like she was a mangy dog, begging for scraps of affection instead of food. But she couldn't stop herself. "Because it's never been remotely like this for me."

Aiden drew in a sharp breath, and goddamnit, she wished she had the guts to look at his face. What did the sound signify?

Shock? Delight?

Disgust?

At last, he leaned over, brushing his lips against her temple. "It's never been like this for me, either. I told you I was done for the second I saw you, and I meant it, Liv. I've never meant anything more in my life."

Grinning like a fool, Olivia rolled on top of him, landing kisses all over his lips, his face, his neck, his chest—any bit of skin she could reach. Aiden squirmed beneath her, laughing as her featherlight kisses tickled his skin, which only spurred her to move faster, to aim for more sensitive spots.

"All right, little minx," Aiden said, flipping her over onto her back, pinning her to the bed with his body. He forced her hands up above her head, his fingers pressing her wrists into the mattress. "I think that's quite enough, thank you."

His gaze was fixed on hers, boring into her, making her feel like he could see straight into her heart. *Love me, love me, love me, love me!* She was desperate for him to see the emotions roaring through her.

"Tell me what you want, Olivia Adams. Take control and make it happen."

She didn't even hesitate. "I want you."

His mouth crashed down over hers, staking his claim as clearly as if he'd tattooed "Property of Aiden" across her chest. Olivia lost herself in the kiss, letting her elation wash through her, filling her near to bursting.

When at last he pulled away, Aiden kept her pinned to the bed, resting his forehead and the tip of his nose against hers. "Oh, Liv. My strong, beautiful girl. I don't know how we're going to make this work, but I'm sure as fuck going to try."

Olivia deflated, ever so slightly. "What do you mean? Why wouldn't it work?"

Lifting his head, he blinked down at her a couple of times. "Well. I mean, it's complicated, isn't it?" When she didn't immediately agree, he rolled onto the mattress beside her, sitting up. She didn't think he meant it, but the way he looked down his nose at her came off condescending as hell, and she pressed her lips into a tight line. "We don't live anywhere near each other. We both have jobs that are important to us, and mine isn't exactly compatible with long-term relationships."

Her mind reeled as she tried to process that. Not compatible with long-term relationships? What the hell? Then why the actual fuck did he bother to ask her what she wanted?

She sat up, too, hugging her knees to her chest. "I don't understand what's going on here."

The sound he made was halfway between frustration and pain. "I'm not saying I don't want to try. Damnit, Liv, I'll try anything for you. I'm just saying it's going to be really fucking hard. It's not like I can pick the Manor up and move it to Boston, and you—"

"I don't give a fuck about Boston," she interrupted. "The only reason I've stayed so long is I never had the guts to find somewhere I liked better."

"Well, okay then. Good." He was picking his words carefully, as if afraid she'd explode at any moment. It grated on her nerves; she wasn't the one saying stupid shit here. "That's one problem solved then. You can move up here. I make more than enough money that you don't even need to work."

Olivia was getting more and more confused every time new words came out of his mouth. "Why wouldn't I work?"

"I'm not saying I'm against you working. I'm not a Neanderthal." He gave a one-shouldered shrug. "I just don't know what you'd do up here. The closest accounting firm of any decent size is probably in Burlington, for Christ's sake. That's an hour and a half away."

"I'm not going to be completely dependent on someone else, Aiden." There was ice in her voice. "Never again in my fucking life."

"Okay, okay." He held up his hands in a placating gesture. "Get whatever job you like. I'm not going to stop you."

Burying her face in her hands, Olivia sighed. What a giant cluster-fuck this was turning out to be. "And I guess you'd never consider leaving the Manor? Finding somewhere new for both of us?"

The room became as quiet and still as a graveyard.

Well, that was her answer then. It wasn't like she was surprised. Fairford Manor wasn't merely a job to him. He'd built the place with his bare fucking hands. It was his whole life.

Maybe too much of his life for there to be enough room left for her.

"It's okay," she said when the silence went on far too long. "It's nice to dream and all, but we're both mature adults. We're perfectly capable of facing reality."

He didn't say anything. But really, what was left to say?

"So again, thank you." She was using the voice she used when talking with difficult clients at work. It made her want to fucking scream. "With everything you've taught me, I'm sure I won't be too afraid to go to a dungeon back home now—find my perfect Dom." She saw him flinch out of the corner of her eye, but pretended she hadn't.

Aiden was quiet for a few moments, his body utterly still. "I hope you find what you're looking for."

"Yeah," Olivia said, closing her eyes against the threat of tears. "Me too."

CHAPTER 15
Aiden

They hadn't said more than a handful of words to each other all morning, and it was making Aiden want to tear his hair out. Was this really how their week together was going to end? With long silences and nervous glances, like a couple of teenagers who lost their virginity on prom night and had no idea what to do about it the next morning?

Though their last joining had been anything but an awkward virginal fumbling. He'd never fucked a woman that way in his life. Hell, did it even really count as fucking? It was worship. A declaration.

It was making love.

The thought stunned him, but he knew beyond a shadow of a doubt it was true. He'd made love to Olivia Adams last night, and he wanted nothing more in the world than to do it again.

Just maybe with more spanking involved next time. That was still making love, right? For people like them?

He had to fix this. Find the words to undo the appalling shitshow he'd made of things last night, and convince her to stay. He'd regret it for the rest of his life if he didn't.

Before he could properly wrap his head around that whole runaway train of thought, Olivia cleared her throat behind him. Dropping the bowl he'd been absentmindedly scrubbing for who-knew-how-long into the sink, he turned to face her.

Olivia stood on the other side of the breakfast bar in leggings and an oversized T-shirt, her suitcase resting at her feet. "I'm all packed," she said, not quite meeting his eyes.

Soapy water dripped from his hands onto the kitchen floor as he stared at her. His mind was completely blank, as though the entire English language had suddenly up and disappeared.

Shifting uncomfortably, Olivia crossed and then immediately uncrossed her arms. "Can you, umm"—she waved a hand in the vague direction of the front door—"give me a ride to my car?"

"Oh," Aiden said, snapping back into his body. He must've looked like an absolute fool. "Right. Of course. Let me grab my keys."

He started to leave the kitchen with his hands still dripping and the faucet going, until Olivia pointed these facts out to him, one corner of her mouth twitching.

How he longed to bend her over one of the breakfast barstools and give her a playful spanking for her sass. Then they could laugh and fuck and talk, and things would be like they'd been most of the rest of the week. It would be perfect again.

But their time was clearly up. And she was ready to go find someone else—her perfect Dom. She'd said so herself.

Aiden rinsed his hands and turned off the water, then cleaned up the floor with a dirty dishtowel. "Anything else I'm forgetting?" he asked, trying to lighten the mood. "I didn't leave the oven on, did I?"

She smiled. "I think you're good."

When they left the house a minute later, Olivia lingered in the doorway, then again in the wildflower garden, looking around as if trying to commit every detail to memory.

Frustration surged up through him, making him clench his hand around his keys, the jagged edges digging into his skin. If she was so fucking reluctant to leave, then why had she packed early? Why had she spent the whole morning avoiding him, then asked for a ride when checkout wasn't until eleven, and it was barely even nine?

Aiden forced himself to take slow, calming breaths. He was being ridiculous. Plenty of guests left a little early on their last day, especially if they had a long way to travel. Olivia had a drive of several hours ahead of her.

Focusing on those logical, rational thoughts, he stowed Olivia's bag in the trunk, climbed behind the wheel, and started the car. The rumble of the engine made her jump, and with a final, fleeting look up at the house, she hurried to join him in the front seat.

"Sorry to keep you waiting," she said as she buckled her seatbelt.

"Not at all."

Their speech was so forced. So stilted. Like two people who'd met only moments before, and wanted to get off on the right foot.

Aiden spent the first ten minutes of their drive wracking his brain, trying to come up with something he could say that would make everything go back to normal. He missed their easy banter and laughter with a desperation that made his chest ache.

For the briefest of moments, he considered ordering her to reach over and pleasure him while he drove—with her hands or even her mouth. Then she could bring herself to completion while he listened to her moans of pleasure.

But no. Everything about her this morning, from her body language to her choice of clothing, made it clear their time together as Dominant and submissive was over.

So when Olivia chose to stare out the windshield and not say a word, he followed her lead. It was his job to make sure she received what she needed, and far be it from him to deny her now, even if it broke him to do it.

It took almost an hour to reach the Manor through the winding mountain roads. Zach must've been watching for them on the security camera, for by the time they'd parked beside Olivia's dark blue Bronco, he was striding across the parking lot.

"Oh, good, he has my keys," Olivia said, climbing out of the car and hurrying over.

"Perfect," Aiden said as she shut the door behind her, not bothering to hide his sarcasm. Like she was listening anyway. Fucking Zach and his fucking efficiency. Now she'd leave even faster.

By the time he forced himself to join them outside, Zach had already loaded her bag into her trunk, and she was giving the receptionist a goodbye hug. "Thank you for everything," she said as they pulled apart. "And for charging my phone! I thought I'd left it in my car all week."

"Aiden gave it to me when you, ahh, *checked in*," he said, giving her an exaggerated wink that made her blush beautifully. "And it was genuinely my pleasure. You've been a delight to have here. And frankly —and very much *off* the record—I'm glad you punched Stacey. She was a nightmare to deal with. I only wish I'd been there to see it."

Olivia's giggle hit him with the force of a sledgehammer to the chest. Christ, he was going to miss her.

"Well, then," Zach said, giving Olivia a silly little bow. "I'll leave you two to say your goodbyes. Safe travels."

"Bye, Zach." She gave a cute little wave. "Thanks again."

Aiden and Olivia stood side-by-side as he walked up the front path, neither of them moving or speaking until he disappeared into the house.

"Well, then," Aiden said, then repressed a cringe. Zach had literally just said that. Wasn't he supposed to be a super suave Dom who swept women right off their feet? He couldn't believe how fucking awkward he was being.

"Well, then," Olivia echoed as she turned to face him, meeting his gaze for the first time since they'd left the cabin. She really did have the most beautiful eyes—a true sapphire blue. He'd never seen quite that shade before.

Desperate for anything to say at all, he pulled out his phone. "I'll send you all the pictures you took," he said, selecting them in his photos app and attaching them to a blank text message. "Here, put in your number."

She took his phone and entered the ten digits quickly, hitting the send button before she handed it back. "Thank you." Her voice was so quiet, as if she was having trouble speaking.

"Of course. I can't very well send you home without all your mush-room pictures."

She cracked a tiny smile. "That would be a real tragedy."

"Liv, I—" His throat was way too tight, and he had to take a moment to compose himself. "I had a wonderful time this week. Don't ever forget how incredible you are."

Stepping forward, she pressed her face against his chest, wrapping her arms tightly around him. His muscles started to relax the moment they were touching again.

"Thank you, Aiden. For everything. I'll never forget you."

And then she was gone, practically fleeing to her car.

Stop her!

The thought repeated in his head over and over, in perfect time with his pounding heart. No matter how urgent it got, though, his feet stayed rooted to the spot as she climbed behind the wheel, fumbling with her keys. The Bronco roared to life, and she was backing up moments later, clearly not wanting to linger.

Don't let her drive away, you fucking idiot!

But that's exactly what he did.

Heart breaking in his chest, he watched her car move down the long driveway. Then her taillights disappeared beyond the front gates, and Olivia was gone.

He stood there for several long minutes, staring at the last place he'd seen her car. It was like his body had forgotten how to move.

When at last his brain was firing on all cylinders again, he made his way slowly toward the lobby, his feet dragging along the flagstones. His toe caught on one of the steps as he climbed onto the porch, and he steadied himself with the railing.

He felt weak. Drained. Like he was on day five of a raging fever.

"So," Zach said as Aiden shouldered his way through the door. "How'd it go?" The man's cocky little smirk was nowhere in sight. And the laugh that always seemed to be right beneath the surface of his voice was gone.

"Not right now." Unable to face the accusation in Zach's eyes, he turned toward the porch. Fuck getting his stuff. Housekeeping would forgive him this once.

With a little tsking sound, Zach muttered, "That's a little dramatic, but you do you, man."

Aiden paused on the threshold, his hands clenched into tight fists at his sides. "I'm not being dramatic," he ground out.

"Forgive me. Walking around like someone just died and storming out of the house are totally normal behaviors for you. My mistake."

Screwing his eyes shut, Aiden made himself take several long, slow breaths. "You wouldn't understand," he said at last.

"Oh, I guarantee you I would," Zach shot back. It was the first time Aiden had ever heard true anger in the man's voice, and he found himself turning around out of sheer surprise.

Zach stood behind the reception counter with his arms crossed tightly over his heathered gray vest, his thin black eyebrows slanted into a furious V.

"I'm sorry," Aiden said, staying by the safety of the front doors. Zach legit looked like he was about ready to take a swing at him. "But I honestly don't know what I did to piss you off."

"You're not the only person here who loves someone they're not supposed to. At least the person you love loves you back. And you're either too stupid or too spineless to do anything about it."

The pain in Zach's voice filled Aiden with shame. It had been more than three years since Zach started working there, and yet he barely knew a thing about the man. Their conversations had always been so superficial.

Or else they'd been about Aiden's problems.

"I'm really sorry." Aiden had to speak around the lump in his throat. "I'm realizing I haven't been a very good friend. But I promise I'll be better if you'll let me."

That placated Zach somewhat. When next he spoke, there was a hint of kindness in his voice. "Thank you. I'd like that." Uncrossing his arms, he shoved his hands in his pockets and sighed. "Sorry for going off on you. I know you've got a lot of shit to deal with right now."

"No, I deserved that." He'd never even asked Zach about his love life, while Zach had to listen to him complain all the time about the various women who came through the Manor's doors. "Do you want to grab a beer and talk about it?"

One corner of Zach's mouth lifted. "I'm not really a *grab a beer with the boys* kind of guy. But thanks for the offer. Besides"—he gave Aiden a pointed look—"I'm a lost cause. You're the one we can fix right here and now."

Leaning back against the doorframe, Aiden groaned. "There's nothing to fix. She's gone. It's over."

"Do you love her?" Zach said it as if the answer was all that mattered.

"Of course I love her," Aiden snapped. "What does that have to do with anything?"

Zach rolled his eyes up toward the vaulted ceiling. "Oh, please."

So much for their temporary truce. "Listen," he said, glaring. "I wish it was that simple. I really do. But I can't offer her the kind of relationship she wants. Not while still working here. And I gave up *everything* for this place. I'm not leaving until I have no fucking choice."

Zach didn't so much as blink at the hostility in his voice. He was cool as a cucumber when he asked, "What kind of relationship does she want?"

"I don't know," Aiden said, getting frustrated again. "A normal one. And there's nothing normal about the Manor."

Arching his brows, Zach asked, "What do you mean by normal? Like, faithful? Did she *ask* you for a monogamous relationship?"

"Yes!" Aiden practically shouted. But then honesty forced him to add, "Sort of. She didn't come right out and say it. But it was implied." Why else would she have said that about leaving the Manor?

Cocking his head to one side, Zach said, "Really? Cause I seem to remember you, Mason, and Camden fucking her three ways from Sunday out by the pool. She didn't appear to mind it all that much."

"Jesus, are you always watching the security feed?" Aiden wasn't sure if he was annoyed or impressed.

Zach shrugged. "Only when there's nothing better to do. But that's not the point. She wants you to share her. *Obviously.* Did you ask her if she's okay sharing you?"

He ran through their conversation from the night before, going over and over every word he could remember. "Not explicitly, no."

"Do you think maybe you . . . *should*? At least then you'll know for sure."

"And if she says no?"

Another shrug. "Then you have to decide which is more important to you. Her or this place." Aiden started to respond, but Zach talked over him. "I know, I know. You gave up everything for the Manor. I don't doubt it. But is it really worth giving up even more? The Manor can never love you back."

Aiden felt like he'd been sucker punched in the gut. There wasn't enough air in the room anymore.

Seeming to think he'd said enough, Zach turned, heading into his little office.

"Wait." Aiden took three long strides across the lobby, the hard soles of his shoes clicking against the marble tiles.

When Zach turned, there were tears glistening in his eyes. He motioned for Aiden to continue.

"What would you do? If you were me, I mean."

The seconds dragged by, Zach opening his mouth a couple times before immediately closing it again. At last, he said, "I'd do anything for the person I love. That's why I stay here, even though I know I'm just torturing myself." Before Aiden could work out what the hell that meant, he slipped the rest of the way into his office, closing the door behind him.

Was Zach in love with someone at the Manor? Someone who didn't return his feelings? It was the only theory that made sense, though he had no idea who it could be.

For the first time, it occurred to him he had no clue what Zach's sexual orientation was; he'd never seen the man act differently around any of the staff or guests. All he knew was the guy liked to watch—and who didn't in a place like this?

Maybe that's why Zach never took any clients. Perhaps he was gay. Or submissive. Or both.

So much to puzzle out, but it would have to wait. Olivia was getting farther and farther away from him by the moment. It was time to figure out what mattered to him most, once and for all.

The Manor can never love you back.

Zach's words were still ringing in his head. Did it mean he'd given up his parents' love for something that could never love him back, too?

No, that wasn't right. His mom and dad had never loved him. Not really. They'd loved the idea of him. The perfect little picture of him in their minds, that he had no chance of ever living up to.

But Olivia loved the real him. The Aiden his parents had rejected.

And he was throwing it all away for an old mansion with pretty woodwork.

Aiden got his cell from his pocket, pulling up his favorites and hitting Leo's name.

"I've been expecting your call," Leo said in lieu of a greeting. "Ever since we all spoke the other night."

Good. Then he didn't have to try explaining. "Do you regret it?" Leo would understand what he was asking.

Did he feel like he gave up on his dream. Like he was missing out. Like choosing Sophie over the Manor had been a mistake.

The sound Leo made then was one of pure contentment. "Not even for a second."

CHAPTER 16

Olivia

Olivia made it about seven and a half of the eight miles to downtown Fairford before she started sobbing. Really, that was rather impressive. She definitely deserved a cookie or a cupcake or something.

No longer able to see, and with hands shaking too much to keep the wheel steady anyway, she pulled over on the side of the deserted road.

"Fuck my fucking life," she said, banging her head back against the headrest. What the ever-loving fuck had she been thinking, going to the Manor? Hadn't she spent the last several years trying to convince Jen she wasn't the kind of person who could handle casual hookups? So, what, it was supposed to be totally different if she *fucking paid for it*? So long as money changed hands, her emotions would be in some sort of magical lockdown?

Olivia let out a wordless scream, trying to shove all her pain and frustration and fear into that single, anguished sound, not stopping until her throat was raw and her lungs demanded air.

Okay, she really needed to get a grip. It was over. Period. End of discussion. Time to get on with her life. And maybe—finally—find someone to share that life with. Someone she was actually allowed to keep.

Wiping her eyes on her sleeves, she grabbed her phone off the passenger seat. She'd been in such a hurry to get away from Aiden before she did something stupid, she hadn't even pulled up directions.

When she brought her phone to life, the top notification (above about a hundred texts and missed calls from Jen, who believed she was at a singles retreat in Florida) was a text from an unknown 802 number —the Vermont area code.

The pictures from Aiden.

It was a bad idea. A *terrible* idea, even. If she was smart, she'd delete it all, block his number, and drive off into the sunset. Figuratively. It was 10:22 in the morning.

But things like self-restraint and intelligence would have to wait for tomorrow.

She pulled up the pictures, going through several angles of the mushrooms she'd found growing on a tree stump. Every time she swiped to the next picture, her heart skipped a beat, knowing what came after the orange and yellow fungus.

At last, she reached the selfies. In the first one, Aiden was stunned— eyes wide, mouth half open, as if someone had smacked him upside the head with a two-by-four. It made her want to laugh and cry at the same time. Swiping her thumb, she pulled up the next picture. The one where he'd wrapped an arm around her and smiled.

Her eyes filled with tears, making his stupid, perfect face blur. The sex and the spankings and the orgasms had, of course, been mind-blowing. But she had a feeling that, in years to come, she'd look back on moments like these the most. Moments when they'd simply been together, talking and laughing, completely happy.

She saved the photo to her phone, then forced herself to move on. She remembered each and every one of the pictures she'd taken on their hike, and her smile was more than a little brittle as she went through them. He'd been so sweet and patient with her, smiling down at her fondly as she flitted around the forest like some sort of wannabe nature photographer.

And there was the unfinished panorama shot she'd taken on the cliff, perfect for about three-quarters of the view, and then a jumbled mess at the end. Her ass literally tingled remembering the belting she got right afterward. She ran a fingertip across her pelvis, where the bark of the fallen tree had been rough and hard against her naked skin.

Olivia couldn't help thinking she'd never find someone who made her feel like that again. Someone who understood her and her needs on an instinctive level, and whose own needs were such a perfect counterpoint to hers.

A person who had built the two most beautiful places in the world. Who made her laugh more in a week than she had the previous thirty-three years of her life. Whose natural inclination was toward kindness, not egotism or cruelty.

With a sigh, she swiped across the screen one more time, pretty sure she'd reached the end. Except there was a single additional picture—one she didn't know Aiden had taken.

It was a picture of herself, standing in front of his cabin. Her back was to him, head turned and slightly down as she studied the explosion of wildflowers. Only a small part of her face was visible, but what she could see looked peaceful, even wistful. As if she hadn't a care in all the world.

Her heartbeat sped up as she studied the little sliver of her own face. She'd never felt that way before this week, let alone seen it in a picture.

And here she was, driving away, as if eternal happiness grew on trees in easy abundance.

"Fuck. This."

Maneuvering out of the picture slideshow, she clicked on Aiden's number and hit call.

He picked up on the first ring. "Liv, I'm—"

"No, fuck this," she interrupted. "We're not just saying it's too hard and giving up. This is fucking real what we have, and I refuse to throw it all away because I'm scared. *Fuck* being scared. I've been scared my entire goddamn life, and it's all sucked until now, and I don't want the rest of it to suck, too.

"I don't fucking care that you're a professional Dom. I think it's hot as hell, frankly. I'm perfectly happy to share you so long as I'm the only one you actually care about, and so long as you share me, too. And I don't give a flying fuck about my job. I never have. I'm going to work because I need to have my own money, but there are a shit ton of remote jobs nowadays. Or maybe we can even find something for me to do at the Manor. I don't fucking know. But I do know we can figure out how to make this work as long as we're not too chickenshit to even try. So this is me fucking trying."

She was out of breath by the time she finished. She sucked air into her lungs as she waited for his response, willing her heart rate to calm down before she had another damn panic attack.

Only he didn't say a word. Not a declaration of love, not a rejection, nothing in between. The only sound was her own breathing as the seconds ticked by.

Fuckity fuck, she'd scared him off. Was he even still on the line? She confirmed the call was still connected. Maybe he was too shocked to speak?

Every single part of her anxiety was telling her to end the call and block his number. It had been stupid to call him, stupider still to say all *that*, and the only way to save face was to spend the rest of her life pretending it had never happened.

Yeah, fuck that, too. The time for hiding under her broken shell, using it as a shield between her and the rest of the world, was over. She'd shot her shot, and that was something to be fucking proud of. Time for him to declare his feelings for her, or else break her heart. At least she'd know.

Swallowing down the lump in her throat, she demanded, "Anything you want to say?"

"Look to your left."

Whipping around, Olivia shrieked as someone appeared right outside her driver's side window. "What the fuck!"

It took a few seconds for the rest of her brain to catch up with the please-don't-murder-me-Mr.-Serial-Killer part, and she realized it was Aiden. With another shout that made him yank the phone away from his ear, Olivia flung her own phone aside and threw open the car door, almost nailing him in the process.

"Aiden!" She shouted his name as she tried to leap out of the car. The seatbelt dug into her hips and chest, making her wince, and she fumbled with the buckle for way too long before she managed to release the fucking thing. Half a heartbeat later, she practically fell out of the

142

car and into his arms. "Oh my God, Aiden, Aiden, Aiden . . ." She was kissing every single part of his face she could reach. "What the fuck are you doing here?"

"Chasing you, obviously," he said, burying his hands in her hair. "About ten minutes after you left, I figured out what a fucking idiot I was being. Which, by the way, Zach will take credit for. But don't listen to him."

Laughing, Olivia went up onto her toes and kissed him properly. She was in control for about a split second before he took over, deepening the kiss, moving them slightly so he could push her up against the back door of her car. His whole body pressed up tightly against hers, one hand clenching her ass like a lifeline. And oh God, how had she ever thought she could live without this. When at last he pulled away, she felt like she was floating ten feet off the ground.

"Good thing you pulled over before you got to town," Aiden said, smiling down at her. "Or the good people of Fairford would've gotten a bit of a show."

"Who cares." Olivia was still breathless from that kiss. "A whole convoy of motorcycles could've gone by, and I wouldn't have noticed."

With a laugh, Aiden said, "Oh, you would've noticed, all right. And it would've made you even hotter."

"I'm not even gonna bother denying it," she said, chuckling, though her laughter died off quickly. "So . . . about all the stuff I said." Goddamn, could her heart beat any faster? "How do you feel about it?"

"As relieved and happy as I've ever been in my life."

"Oh, thank fuck," she muttered, making him laugh again.

"You're right, Liv, about all of it. We can make this work. We *have* to. We just need to trust each other enough to be honest—which we've both clearly been too fucking scared to do for the last several days. That's got to end now if we want any chance of working through the bumps in the road." His expression turned more serious. "Because they're going to come up. This isn't an easy life we're trying to build here. But Christ, I don't want a life without you in it. That sounds like pure fucking torture to me. And I'll do every single thing in my power to make sure we figure this out so we're both truly happy."

She smiled at him. "Happily ever after?"

"Something like that." He ran a thumb over her bottom lip. "I hope this isn't too much too soon but . . . I love you, Liv. I don't ever want to let you go."

Tears slipped from her eyes. "I love you, too. And you already know I'm yours."

Brushing the hair out of her face, Aiden leaned down to skim his lips against hers. "Come on, love. Let's go home."

EPILOGUE

Olivia

Six Months Later

"S hit." Olivia threw her car into park and turned off the ignition. The clock read 4:59, and Aiden had told her to be at the Manor no later than five if she wanted to avoid a punishment.

The last thing she wanted on her own birthday was a real punishment.

She ran toward the front door, praying there wasn't any ice on the pathway, still fighting her disappointment that Aiden had needed to work all afternoon. Her birthday had fallen on a Sunday this year, so would it have really been so hard to have his newest guest check in on Monday instead? And he even wanted her to meet him at the Manor. As far as she was concerned, they spent enough of their time at work as it was.

Though Aiden had cut back a lot, wanting to spend more time with her; most of his guests booked for five days now instead of seven, and he never spent the night at the Manor, no matter what.

At first, Olivia had been worried she'd get jealous when he went off to work. That she'd sit at home in their cabin, stewing about the women he was fucking and spanking instead of her.

She'd told him she wouldn't, of course. She'd even believed it at the time. It still came as one hell of a relief when it turned out to actually be true.

The first time he'd headed off to work and left her behind, she'd spent half the day imagining what he was up to, unable to stop touching herself. When he got home, Aiden had given her ten with a paddle for each and every orgasm she'd had without his permission, and then fucked her senseless.

As for Olivia, her lifetime ban from Fairford Manor had lasted about the lifespan of a gnat. She was now their official accountant and bookkeeper—something that made Zach extremely happy, as his relationship with math was patchy at best. She'd even been a third in a couple of scenes, which had been spectacularly thrilling to say the least.

The last six months had been more wonderful than she could've possibly hoped. Her only complaints had to do with Aiden abandoning her for several hours on her birthday—and that the parking lot was so fucking far from the front door. Olivia was gasping for breath as she bounded up the front steps and into the lobby.

"Just in time," Zach said, giving his watch a pointed look.

"Tell him," Olivia said, pausing to suck more air into her lungs while she hung up her coat. She moved farther away from the front door, trying to rub some life back into her freezing arms. It was only a few degrees above zero out there. "Tell him I wasn't late."

Shoulders shaking with silent laughter, Zach fished his phone out of his pocket and shot off a text. "There," he said. "You're safe."

"Thanks." She flashed him a grateful smile. "You're the best."

Zach's answering grin was full of mischief. "You'd better hurry up anyway. You know they don't like to be kept waiting."

Her eyebrows shot upward at the speed of light. "They?"

He gave her something resembling an apologetic smile, though he obviously didn't feel bad in the least. "Sorry, honey. I promised not to say a word." He winked at her. "They're in the game room."

"Oh, no." She planted her hands on her hips. "If this was a party, you'd be staying. I want to know what Aiden's got planned." When he

146

didn't respond, she added, "You may have known them longer, but you know me *better*." None of the Doms had even gotten to know Zach well enough to realize he was gay, for fuck's sake. Though Mason swore he'd suspected.

But it was no use. With one final, downright evil grin, he grabbed his wool peacoat and waltzed out the front door, calling, "Enjoy your birthday!" over his shoulder.

"Motherfucker," she muttered under her breath, gazing after him. He could've at least given her a tiny little clue.

Oh, well. Even with Zach's text, she didn't want to push her luck by taking her time. Straightening the red satin of her dress and running her fingers once through her wild mane of hair, she set off down the back hallway.

The clack of pool balls and murmur of voices drifted down the hall, reaching her ears well before she reached the doorway. If only she hadn't worn heels. It would've been nice to take a second to steel her nerves, but there was no way they hadn't heard her coming. With a final deep breath, she stepped into the room.

"Oh, fuck." The words were out of her mouth before she could stop them.

Five pairs of eyes turned in her direction at once.

"That better not be disappointment I hear," Camden said, grinning at her. The other four seemed less amused by her entrance.

"Not at all," she said, doing her best to appear meek and apologetic. "Just surprise. That's all." Meanwhile, her thoughts were in a jumble as she tried to figure out what the fuck Aiden was up to that involved every Dom in the Manor. They were even all wearing suits—normal garb for Jonathan and Mason, but the rest? Jesus fuck, they were sexy as hell.

Aiden kept up his stern Dom look for a few more seconds, then he must've decided to go easy on her for her birthday. With a warm smile, he put down his pool cue and crossed the room, folding her into his arms. "I missed you, love," he whispered into her hair.

"I missed you, too." She breathed deeply, his woodsmoke and mountain air smell even stronger now it was winter. Fuck, he smelled so good. How was she already three seconds away from licking him?

Pulling away before she did something embarrassing, she asked, "Where are all the guests?"

"There aren't any," Aiden said, grinning as her jaw dropped.

The others moved up to form a circle around her. "Last week's guests checked out yesterday, and this week's won't arrive until tomorrow afternoon," Jonathan told her. "Fairford Manor is officially closed, for one night only."

Had they really done all this for her? She should've known Aiden wouldn't abandon her on her birthday without a very good reason.

"Now," Aiden said, turning her around and holding her against him, his chest warm and hard against her back. "Are you ready for your birthday surprise?"

Olivia smiled. "Yes, Sir."

"Good girl. Mason, if you would."

Reaching into his pocket, Mason pulled out a folded rectangle of cloth. Gripping one corner, he let the rest tumble toward the floor, revealing a black silk blindfold.

Her heart was racing as Aiden passed her to the other Dom, and he slipped the soft fabric over her eyes, tying a tight knot behind her head. He trailed his fingers down the long tails of the blindfold, continuing down the center of her back to her zipper. He lowered it slowly, inch by painstaking inch, letting her build herself up into a near-frenzy with excitement. One of the others pushed the straps from her arms, and the dress slipped down her body to the floor.

"*Very* nice," Rafe said.

She blushed furiously, but couldn't hold back a pleased smile. She'd ordered all new lingerie to surprise Aiden, including a lace garter belt and stockings. Standing up a little straighter, she arched her back slightly, feeling as beautiful as she'd ever felt in her life.

Someone traced a fingertip along the cups of her black lace bustier, while another hand brushed across the lacy top of her stockings. Goosebumps erupted across her skin, and her nipples hardened into aching peaks.

"We'd planned to strip you naked," Mason said, and she suspected he was the one tugging on her thong, teasing her with the thin strip of fabric.

"But this . . ." Jonathan pinched her nipple through the thin lace.

"This is far too beautiful to remove just yet," Aiden finished for him. He cupped her face between his hands—the only warning she got before he kissed her.

Olivia melted against him, letting him take ownership of her mouth while the others continued to explore her body. Yeah, this was already better than her previous thirty-three birthdays combined.

When they all pulled away as one, leaving her breathless, she reached out blindly, desperate for more contact. "Please," she said, her voice a little shaky.

"Don't worry." Aiden was behind her now, scooping her up into his arms. "We've got you. All of us."

"Where are we going?" she asked as he carried her from the room.

Camden chuckled. "Inquisitive little thing, isn't she?"

"You have no idea," Jonathan said with a dramatic sigh. She'd scened with him and a guest a few weeks before, and he'd gotten so tired of her constant stream of babble that he'd gagged her.

She shivered at the memory.

Before Olivia could ask about their destination again, she heard the all-too-familiar click of the dungeon door unlocking. Oh, fuck yes. Things were about to get good.

As they filed down the stairs, the bass beat of the music vibrated through her. She had no idea where they managed to find such perfect music all the time—what was this, track twelve on *Sexy Sex Dungeon Music, Vol. 4*? All she knew was it managed to put her in the perfect submissive headspace within seconds, every single time.

When Aiden set her down at last, she was seated on the edge of something, her legs dangling. She felt around with her hands, and guessed she was perched on top of some kind of padded bondage table.

"Be good," Aiden said, taking hold of her wrists and folding her hands in her lap.

Then there were more hands on her, removing her high heels, undoing the clasps on her bustier and trailing the straps slowly down her arms. There was the snip of scissors, and her brand new thong was whisked away. Unable to stop herself, she made a disappointed little sound.

Chuckling, Aiden said, "I'll replace it, Liv. I promise."

Oh. Well then. That was a horse of a different color. Especially since they left her garter belt and stockings on. She'd spent a good twenty minutes admiring herself in the bathroom mirror after she'd put them on that afternoon. It felt good to know she wasn't the only one who thought they made her look sexy as fuck.

When at last they removed the blindfold, even the low lighting of the dungeon was dazzling to her eyes. She blinked several times, until all the black spots disappeared.

The five men were arranged around her, Mason and Jonathan on her right, Camden and Rafe on her left. Aiden stood behind her, his hands resting where her shoulders met her neck.

She'd been correct about the bondage table. In fact, it was her favorite piece of furniture in the dungeon—the one she'd noticed the first time Aiden took her down there, with at least twenty D-Rings spaced evenly around the edge. An assortment of leather straps, cuffs, and chains were arranged neatly below her feet, waiting to bind her to the table in any of a hundred ways.

And that wasn't even what made her the wettest. Beyond the straps and cuffs was a long, narrow table with five implements on its surface: riding crop, paddle, belt, flogger, and three-ply slapper, all in black leather. Each had a small black tent card in front of it, the numbers one through five written on them in silver ink. Olivia recognized Zach's perfect calligraphy from the acceptance letters he mailed out each week.

"You've been such a good girl this year," Aiden said, his thumbs stroking the side of her neck. "I wanted to give you something special for your birthday. Something you'd never forget."

She licked her lips excitedly. "Do I get to choose?"

Several of them laughed, and Camden said, "Oh, baby. There are five of them and five of us. What do you think?"

Her eyes widened. "*All* of them?"

"I was originally planning a more traditional birthday spanking," Aiden said, his hands now circling her neck but exerting no pressure. It was making it hard for her to focus. "Thirty-four licks over my knee and all of that. But it was too predictable. So in order to spice things up a bit, I invented a little game for you to play."

Olivia squirmed, certain she was leaving a wet spot on the leather table. "What kind of game, Sir?"

In answer, Jonathan reached into his pocket and held out two dice —one black and one white. "Roll the dice and find out."

Her hand trembling slightly with excitement, she plucked the two dice from his palm. Good lord, this was the most deliciously terrifying thing she'd ever done. After a single quick shake, she rolled the dice onto the table.

The white die read five, the black die four.

"Fuck yes," Camden said, grinning. He picked up the flogger, running the two dozen or so falls through his fingers.

"So the black die is for which implement you get to use," Olivia said, eyeing the number four tent card in front of the flogger's now-empty spot. "Is the white one which of you uses it?"

Camden was shaking his head before she even finished. "No, we drew straws before you got here to figure out the order. The white die tells me where I get to fuck you."

Olivia was pretty sure her blood legit heated several degrees. Aiden had gotten her a gangbang for her birthday. She had to be the luckiest goddamn woman in the world.

"Evens for pussy, odds for mouth," Aiden said, as Camden made his choices from the straps and cuffs. His fingers tightened possessively against her throat. "Only I get to fuck you in the ass, Liv."

Oh, sweet fuck. She was already about half a second away from having an orgasm, and they hadn't even *done* anything yet. "I get to come as many times as I want, right?" It was more a plea than a question. "Since it's my birthday?"

Jonathan and Mason gave each other an amused look, and Rafe leered down at her with a wolfish smile. "You didn't tell me how greedy she is," Rafe said.

"She's usually much better behaved," Aiden said indulgently, kissing the top of her head. "Though I think I'll let her be greedy, just this once. It is her birthday, after all."

"Soft." Rafe shook his head. "Too soft." He sounded entertained rather than annoyed, though.

Camden stood, having made his selections. "Let's get you warmed up with something simple. Lie on your belly for me."

Several seconds ticked by before Aiden finally relinquished his grip on her neck. She missed the sensation immediately. But not wanting to disappoint any of them, she didn't say a word, instead flipping down onto her stomach.

Camden took hold of her upper arms, shifting her all the way forward on the table, until her chin hung over the edge. Then he used three long straps to bind her, clipping the ends into the D-Rings and adjusting them until they were perfectly tight. The straps across her shoulder blades and waist pinned her arms to her sides, and the third strap cut across her calves.

She tried to wriggle around, and was delighted there was very little give. The only thing she could do was open her legs the tiniest bit.

"First, your birthday spanking," Camden announced, as if he was the emcee at a grand party. "Count them for me, baby."

Olivia loved floggers. In her opinion, they were the most versatile spanking implement of them all. When wielded by a more severe Dom, the pain could be excruciating—especially if the falls were made of braided leather. In Camden's hand, though, the soft leather flicked against her ass with enough force to have a scintillating bite, but not really hurt.

Her voice got more and more eager as she called out each number. Every once in a while, some of the tails would flick down between her legs, and she longed for them to reach her pulsing clit. She strained against the leather strap across her legs, desperate to give him better access, but it was no use. By the time she called out number thirty-four, she was sure her ass was a soft, rosy pink, and the ache in her pussy made her want to cry.

"Please."

Putting the flogger aside, Camden reached between her thighs, pumping two fingers into her pussy. "She's fucking drenched." He sounded like he was bragging. "Someone want to get her off while I fuck her mouth? I don't think she can take much more before she implodes."

Rafe made a low rasp of disapproval. "Haven't you ever heard of edging?"

Olivia's wail was involuntary. "Oh God, please don't. You said I've been a good girl this year!"

Chuckling, Aiden moved up beside her. "Don't worry, love. I've got you." And as Camden moved into place at the head of the table, her own Dom stepped up beside her, trailing his fingers across her punished ass, heightening the sweet sting. "Be a good girl and suck Camden off, and I'll make sure you're rewarded for it."

Olivia parted her lips eagerly as Camden undid his zipper and pulled his cock free. Goddamn, she'd forgotten how huge he was. Thank fuck she'd had plenty of practice over the last several months, and had finally learned to relax her throat.

Taking hold of her face with both hands, Camden got her into the position he wanted. As soon as he thrust his cock into her mouth, Aiden started rubbing slow, firm circles against her clit. She tried to suck and swirl her tongue, wanting to give Camden as much pleasure as possible, but fucking hell, Aiden's fingers were too distracting.

Camden didn't seem to mind anyway. His hands were buried in her hair, holding her at the right angle as he fucked her face mercilessly. It took every bit of concentration she could spare simply to breathe during those brief, fleeting moments when air was possible.

"Jesus . . . *Christ*," Camden ground out, his hands tightening in her hair.

At the same time, Aiden sped up his own ministrations, sending her hurtling toward the edge. She cried out around Camden's cock as her orgasm exploded over her, and he came moments later, the salty taste of his come hitting the back of her tongue.

Before the aftershocks even ended, the straps were removed and she was sitting up on the table, two dice in her hand. She rolled double fives that time.

With a satisfied smile, Mason picked up the slapper. It had three layers in different lengths, each about two inches wide. Tucking it into his belt, he took hold of Olivia, using a firm grip on her shoulder and a hand under her legs to manhandle her into his desired position.

By the time he was finished with her, she was on her back, head dangling upside down off the edge of the table, her long hair trailing down toward the floor. He'd bent her legs so far back her knees pressed against her chest, then cuffed her ankles and wrists together up in midair. The cuffs were chained to D-Rings to either side of her face, making it impossible to lower her legs.

"Lovely," Mason said, trailing the slapper down the back of her stockinged thigh. "There will be no need to count."

The triple impact of the slapper, each layer thudding against her skin a split second after the one before, made her cry out in excitement rather than pain. The way he had her positioned, she was on lewd display, and he alternated between strokes, her bottom on one, her pussy and clit the next.

"Fuuuuuuuck," she said the fifth time he brought the slapper down on her clit. And he wasn't even a third of the way through. She didn't know how she'd survive the rest without going to absolute pieces.

"Does your Dom let you talk like that, little girl?" Mason demanded, giving a particularly harsh stroke across her ass.

She yelped, her muscles straining against the chains. "O-only when I'm not in trouble, Sir," she answered, her breath coming in rapid spurts. Sweet fucking Jesus, it felt so fucking good.

Tsking, he said, "You're lucky you don't belong to me." And then he was back at it with greater vigor, the impacts harder and closer together.

Olivia wasn't sure what she said after that, but she was confident none of it met Mason's approval. And she was fairly sure she committed several acts of blasphemy when she came.

She was still flying high when Mason pried her lips open with his thumbs and pushed into her mouth. It felt so perfectly deviant to suck a cock upside down, his balls slapping against her face with each thrust. Closing her eyes, she lost herself in the feeling of being used, loving every goddamn second of it.

When he was finished, Mason gently wiped the come from her lips before releasing her.

Two down, three to go. She had no idea how she was going to survive it.

Aiden placed the dice back in her hand. She had to roll the black one twice before she got a new number. The white die was finally even.

It was Rafe who grabbed the riding crop from the small table. She knew he would've preferred a cane—his favorite implement for inflicting pain. But after a long discussion with Aiden, she'd added that to her list of hard limits following the one time he'd used it on her. It had been more pain than she could handle, and rather than push her deeper into submission, it only made her panic.

Rafe put her on her elbows and knees, wrists and ankles cuffed to the edges of the table, ass high in the air. It was one of her favorite positions, and her pussy clenched all on its own.

"I'm less lenient than the others," he said, gripping her hair and craning her neck back. "Since you can't control that dirty little mouth of yours, I'll have to gag it."

Her eyes fluttered closed as he pushed a black silicone ball gag between her teeth. She obediently clamped her mouth around it and lowered her forehead to the table, so he could buckle the strap behind her head.

"Finally, some obedience out of you." He trailed the crop's flat leather slapper through her slit, the edge rough and hard against her sensitive skin. "If you come without permission this time, I don't care what Aiden says. You *will* be punished. Do you understand me?"

She made a noise of assent around the gag.

"Good. Now let's begin."

It was a good fucking thing he gagged her, because he must not have gotten the memo that her birthday spankings were for pleasure, not pain. Her ass was dancing in the air after only three strokes.

Rafe took firm grip of her hips, holding her in place. "Be still, or I'll go even harder." It was a promise, not a threat.

Screwing her eyes closed, Olivia nodded. Every single muscle in her body was tense as she waited for the next stroke to fall.

Slap.

Jesus fucking fuck, it hurt so much.

Slap, slap, slap.

It kept going, one stroke after the other, Rafe never even giving her a moment to collect herself or settle into the pain. She was crying by stroke twenty, straight up sobbing by twenty-five. She knew her face was a disgusting mess of tears and snot and drool.

But her ass stayed exactly where he wanted it all the way through to the end.

"Good girl," Rafe said, kneeling up on the table behind her. "For that, you've earned the right to come."

And then he was fucking her, and fucking hell, she'd never scened with Rafe before, and wasn't prepared for the way he pounded into her like her pussy owed him money. After a few minutes, he switched up his angle, and she whined around the gag as he hit her G-spot over and over.

So. Fucking. Good.

She came first, new tears springing to her eyes at the intensity of it, her clenching pussy sending him over the edge with her.

Was she really supposed to do this two more times? Was that even possible? Her body felt so utterly used and spent, she couldn't imagine anyone being able to wring any more pleasure out of her.

Rafe was surprisingly gentle as he released her and got her cleaned up, taking special care to wipe her face clean with a soft cloth. "I'm glad we finally got to do this," he said, and good heavens, he was actually smiling. "I hope you can be a third in some of my scenes in the future."

As long as he respected her hard limit on canes, that could definitely be arranged.

Once again, she had to roll the black die multiple times, until it finally landed on six. "What happens now?" she asked, eyeing the little black tent cards, which only went up to five.

"Wielder's choice," Jonathan said with great satisfaction. Picking up the belt, he bent it double and snapped the two sides together. One corner of his mouth lifted at the loud *crack* it made. "I'm glad I get to fuck your pussy. After all, I've already had your mouth."

She blushed a deep crimson, relishing in the shiver running down her spine. "I'm glad, too, Sir."

Jonathan got her to her feet, leading her to the foot of the table. "Aiden's told me how much you love being bent over the furniture," he said, pushing between her shoulder blades.

Sighing contentedly, she bent at the waist until her stomach, breasts, and cheek were pressed against the smooth leather. She stayed perfectly still as Jonathan bound her to the table, cuffing her ankles to the table legs and using a single, wide strap across her waist.

"Hands at the small of your back," he ordered, cuffing them together when she complied.

She turned her head so she could see Aiden, watching her with so much love and pride that her heart swelled. "Thank you," she said, her voice more than a little dreamy.

Aiden brushed her hair behind her ear. "Keep being a good girl for Jonathan. I'm next, love."

Olivia's legs were shaking before the belt even touched her. She'd been bent and twisted and contorted like some sort of fucked-up doll, and her muscles were growing weaker by the moment. Once Jonathan got started, she sagged against the table, letting her torso support most of her weight. He focused his effort on the tender flesh of her thighs, though she could tell he was holding back most of his strength. The soft bite of pain was enough to make her skin warm and tingly.

She kept her gaze locked with Aiden's through all thirty-four strokes.

When at last Jonathan tossed the belt aside and positioned himself between her spread thighs, Aiden pressed two fingers against her lips. "Suck," he ordered, pushing them into her mouth. "And use plenty of spit, because that's all the lube you're getting before I start finger-fucking your ass."

With an excited moan, she put her all into sucking his fingers, laving them with her tongue, making them as wet as she possibly could. She was sucking so hard that when he pulled his fingers from her mouth, they made a wet *pop*.

She didn't know which hands belonged to whom, but one gripped her hip possessively, while two others spread her ass cheeks wide apart, baring all of her. As Aiden pushed his fingers into her ass, Jonathan entered her slowly from behind in one long, fluid stroke.

Olivia moaned again, closing her eyes. The two Doms worked her pussy and ass in perfect tandem, matching each other's rhythm. One of them reached down to tease her clit, too, and she found herself begging for them to stop. "Too much," she said over and over, her voice trembling as much as the rest of her. "Please no. It's way too much. I can't, I can't, I *ca-a-a-a-an't*."

Thank fucking God they didn't listen.

157

When she came, it actually hurt. The muscles in her abdomen seized up so violently she screamed. But pain mixed with bliss was her favorite feeling of all.

Aiden and Jonathan worked together to release her. Once all the straps and cuffs were removed, she was too tired to stand, instead letting her arms flop lifelessly to her sides.

"I'm going to die," she said, letting herself be as dramatic as she deserved.

Leaning over her, Aiden massaged her shoulders and back, easing some of the tension in her poor, abused muscles. "You're breathtaking, Liv," he said, something very like awe in his voice. "Watching you tonight has been one of the best experiences of my life. Do you think you'll be able to finish the scene? For me?"

Olivia was fairly sure those words would've brought her out of a coma. Dredging up reserves of strength she didn't know she had, she pushed off the table and stood.

"My good girl," Aiden said, helping her climb up onto the table on her knees, her feet hanging over the edge. "Bend all the way over for me, and stretch your arms forward as far as they can go."

She did as she was told, hissing at the extreme stretch in her already abused thigh muscles when he pushed her ass down, so her bottom rested on her heels. He bound her to the table like that, one strap across her shoulder blades, the other at the small of her back, cinching the backs of her thighs and calves together. Her wrists went into cuffs, which he chained to the front of the table, tight enough to make her shoulders ache.

Olivia really needed to start doing some yoga.

"You're perfect," he said, and she lifted her head in time to see him pick up the final implement: the black leather paddle.

Lowering her forehead to the table, she tried to loosen her muscles. Aiden loved it when she was relaxed for him.

"Thirty-four for my beautiful birthday girl," he said, running the smooth surface of the paddle against her already sensitive skin.

He took it easy on her for the first thirty, for which she would be eternally grateful. Not only did he spread the strokes around, he also only hit with enough force to leave a mild tingling behind after each impact. It was the warm, wonderful kind of pain that would've had her panting if she wasn't so exhausted.

For the last four, though, he pulled out all the stops. She screamed more from shock than the actual pain as the paddle slammed into the center of her left cheek. When it came down just as hard in the center of her right, her body desperately tried to rock forward to lessen the impact. But there was zero give in the straps tying her down.

The final two came one right after the other, in the exact same spots. All the breath left her lungs with a loud *whoosh*, and it took several seconds to remember how to breathe.

"Such a good girl," Aiden crooned as he rubbed her swollen flesh. "You've certainly earned your birthday ass fucking."

Olivia whimpered. Even as sore and exhausted as she was, hearing him talk about taking her in the ass did something magical to her at her very core.

"But first, something special for you."

There was the tear of tape—*Fucking tape? Really?*—and then something hard and smooth was pressed against her clit. A second later, he pressed the tape firmly against her soft, waxed skin, securing what she assumed was a bullet vibrator in place.

No, he wouldn't do that to her. Not after everything he'd already put her body through.

Oh, but he absolutely fucking did. There was a soft *click*, and then the tiny bit of silicone started vibrating. It took everything in her not to sob at the sweet agony of it.

He pushed into her slowly, his lubed cock sliding past her tight ring with little resistance. Once he was fully within her, he paused, reaching down to make sure the vibrator was still exactly where he wanted it. "Fly for me, love. One more time." And then he gave her the ass fucking of a lifetime.

Strapped down as she was, all she could do was moan as he pounded into her, the vibrator forcing her to climb higher and higher, until it was pain instead of pleasure. Every muscle was clenched so tightly, her whole body was vibrating along with the tiny bullet. If she didn't come soon, her body was literally going to break.

At last, the vibrator pushed her over the edge, and it was the most exquisite pain she'd ever felt in her life. Rather than waves crashing over her, it was like being bashed against the shore. "Please make it stop!" She screamed it, her voice raw with desperation.

Aiden pulled out completely, ripping the tape away a moment later. Relief flowed through every single cell in her body, wrenching a single sob from her throat. Before she could even begin to recover, Aiden's hot come was landing on her back and the top of her ass.

A sense of profound peace settled over Olivia. It felt like he was branding her, not wanting anyone to forget who she belonged to. "Thank you," she muttered, so quietly she doubted anyone heard her. "Thank you, Sir."

There was a whirlwind of movement after that, and Olivia was far too tired to pay attention to any of it. All she knew was she wasn't strapped down to the table anymore, and Aiden had carried her over to a couch against one of the dungeon walls. She was fairly certain someone had wiped her clean, but she didn't care enough to reach around and check.

It was a while before she had the strength to open her eyes again. She may have even fallen asleep for a while, though if she had, the others didn't seem to mind.

Olivia found herself sideways in Aiden's lap, his arms holding her tight against him, her head nestled into the crook of his neck. Camden sat beside them, her feet on his lap. As soon as she stirred, he began giving her a heavenly foot massage. The other three were arranged around them in folding chairs; they must've brought them down earlier in the day, for she'd never seen them in the dungeon before.

"You were perfect," Aiden said, filling her with joy.

"Thank you." She took extra care to make sure it was audible this time. "All of you. This is the best birthday I've ever had."

All five of them beamed at her.

"It's not over yet," Aiden said softly, his lips brushing against her ear. "I have one more present for you."

Olivia groaned. "Oh, fuck me. Please say you're joking. I will literally die if you're not joking."

"Don't worry," Aiden said, rubbing soothing circles on her back. "That part of the night is over. I promise. This is something else."

Camden reached behind him, then handed Aiden a present wrapped in bright paper, an elaborate yellow bow on top. She almost asked for permission to open it in the morning. All she wanted to do was sleep. But everyone was watching her so intently, and she couldn't disappoint them.

Forcing her lips into a smile, she took the present, carefully removing the pretty paper and setting it aside. It was a wooden box, about the size of a hardcover book, carved with images of nature—leaves, flowers, and even several perfectly detailed little mushrooms.

Her smile came naturally after that. "It reminds me of our hike," she said, running her fingertip over the carvings. "It's beautif—"

Olivia forgot what she was saying. Aiden had reached down and opened the box.

Inside, nestled in a bed of black silk, was a thin circlet of white gold. *A collar.*

She couldn't take her eyes off it.

"Olivia Adams," Aiden said, plucking the collar from its box, undoing the tiny clasp, "I love you more than I'm ever going to be able to say. But I'd very much love to spend the rest of my life trying. There's not a thing in my life that matters without you, and not a single thing you don't make better by being mine. I only hope you'll consent to be mine forever. Will you marry me?"

Tears slid down her cheeks as she looked up into his eyes. "*Yes.*" It was the easiest answer she'd ever given. "You're everything to me, Aiden. There's nothing in this world I want more than to be bound to you forever." The others clapped and wolf whistled as he fastened the stiff metal collar around her neck.

Reaching up, she ran a fingertip along the cool metal. The feel of it against her throat—a constant reminder of who she belonged to—was like the final piece of a puzzle, clicking perfectly into place.

For the first time in her life, she felt truly whole.

The End

Acknowledgments

Endless thanks to Robin Johnson at Covers by Robin (www. gobookcoverdesign.com) for my absolutely gorgeous cover art. To Shari Ryan at MatHat Studios for my beautiful interior formatting. To my editor, Misha Robinson at Verity Ink Editorial. To my proofreader, Virginia Carey. And to Karen Washo at Utterly Unashamed for completely rewriting my blurb and making it shine.

Special thanks go out to Linda Russell and the rest of the team at Foreword PR & Marketing for the eighty-seven million things you've done for me. You helped make a scary and sometimes stressful process exciting and fun, and I can't thank you enough for your brilliance and expertise.

Last but certainly not least, thank you to my husband Jason, who has supported my dream to be a published author from the day we met. Through nearly two decades of ups and downs, weeks-long writing and editing binges, and finally a major swerve into writing romance, you've been there doing everything you could to help me keep going. I love you as big as the whole universe.

About the Author

Bay Sinclair is the author of steamy romance with broken girls, sexy Doms, and lots of heart. She writes contemporary romance—though she was one credit away from a history minor in college, and historical romances hold a special place in her heart. When she isn't writing, she's an avid foodie in search of the next great culinary adventure, and she drinks entirely too much green tea.

Connect Online
BaySinclair.com

 facebook.com/100092035117400

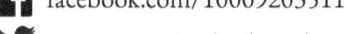 twitter.com/authorbsinclair

 instagram.com/authorbsinclair

www.ingramcontent.com/pod-product-compliance
Lightning Source LLC
Chambersburg PA
CBHW020640250626
47154CB00008B/2763